Cowboys Are A Separate Species

"If cowboys are human, they're sure a separate species."
—Charles M. Russell

Cowboys
Are A
Separate Species

JOHN R. ERICKSON

Illustrations by Gerald L. Holmes

Maverick Books

The articles in this collection first appeared in *The Dallas Times-Herald* and *The Livestock Weekly* between 1977 and 1985, some in slightly different form.

International Standard Book Number: 0-916941-18-3 (paper)
International Standard Book Number: 0-916941-19-1 (cloth)

Second printing, 1991

Maverick Books
P.O. Box 549
Perryton, Texas 79070
(806) 435-7611

This one is for Jim and Marilyn Gregg of Beaver City

Introduction

This is a collection of short pieces I wrote between 1976 and 1985, and which appeared in *The Dallas Times-Herald* and *The Livestock Weekly*.

Most of the pieces come from my experiences as a cowboy in the Texas and Oklahoma Panhandles, and all of them reflect a cowboy's way of looking at the world.

Charlie Russell was right in saying that cowboys are a separate species, but in today's world we could take it a step farther and say that anyone who lives beyond the glow of city lights belongs to a separate species.

In our small towns and RFD communities, we cling to a way of life that was tested by our parents and grandparents. It has its flaws but it has taken us through two world wars, two undeclared wars, the economic cataclysm of the 1930s, and several long dry spells. That's not a bad record.

One of the ingredients in our way of looking at the world is a good, stout sense of humor. It keeps us humble and gives us a tonic against the chaos of ranching, parenthood, and other bad habits. In a few of these pieces, I put on a long face and talk of serious matters, but most of them were written for fun.

I should know better than to write about politics or religion or the silliness of our age, yet every now and then I get on a snort and have to go a few rounds. Most of my writing of that type goes to the Perryton city dump, where it belongs, but I have judged a few of them good enough to include here.

We can all hope that the Perryton city dump is never opened up by archeologists of some future age. They would get a very bad impression of Texas in the twentieth century.

Perryton, Texas
January, 1986

Contents

Summer Cowboy

In 1974 I was managing the Crown Ranch northeast of Beaver, Oklahoma, 5000 acres of sandhills and sagebrush broken here and there by flats of tight buffalo grass country.

I had been hired by the trust department of a bank to manage the ranch, and although I had worked ranches since I was old enough to choose between cowpunching and piano lessons, this was my first executive position.

I had it all to myself. During the spring and fall roundups, I swapped out help with the neighbors and dayworked a few cowboys from town, but the rest of the time Kristine and I did it all.

That first summer, one of my goals was to work over every windmill and water tank on the place. The ranch had no creeks or springs, so maintaining the water supply was a rather crucial part of my job. I could have messed up the horseback work, but I didn't dare run out of water.

Every well on the place needed to be re-leathered and have the top and bottom checks filed down and dressed. Much of the jet rod was pencil-thin and needed to be replaced, and some of the tanks had silted up so badly that they didn't hold much water.

It happened that I had a cousin living in Houston at that time, a skinny sophomore in high school with soft unbearded cheeks and a mop of hair that hung down to his shoulders.

Andy was a good solid kid but very definitely a teenager. He enjoyed racing motorcycles and listening to loud music, and he had a teenage boy's natural aversion to any kind of productive activity.

Well, I needed a summer cowboy, and Andy's folks thought it wouldn't hurt him to get away from Houston and all its evil influences, so we struck a deal.

They indentured Andy to me for the summer, and I talked the trust department into paying him a little salary.

Every day for the next month or so, Andy and I were in the windmill business. We replaced the top checks and bottom checks and put them back in with new leathers. We threw out all the old jet rod and replaced it with new.

We tightened the fan bolts, replaced bad fan sections and tail springs, oiled the heads, and fixed the fan brakes, so that a guy could shut off a mill without climbing the tower and sticking his hand into the spokes.

And while we were doing all this, we had syphon tubes going, draining the water out of the tanks, so that when we got the mill put back together, we stripped down to our undies, grabbed scoop shovels and buckets, and plunged into that awful, sulphur-smelling black gunk that collects in the bottom of a stock tank.

It all went over the side: gunk, mud, moss, cattails, salamanders, waterbugs, everything down to the cement. In some of the tanks the cattails roots were so thick, we had to chop them out with an axe and throw them out in big chunks.

Sweat streamed down our faces and backs, and in the stillness of mid-day we had plenty of company: mosquitoes and biting flies and yellowjacket wasps. You could see where we had been bitten. Every spot was marked by a muddy hand print where we'd slapped at them.

By the time we got back to the house after one of these sessions, we smelled like something dead on the side of the road. We had to bathe in the stock tank down at the barn before Kris would let us in the house to bathe again.

2

Andy stayed right in there and made a hand, but after a couple of weeks he began to wonder about this "cowboy" work. What happened to the old notion that cowboys rode horses and punched cattle? Rounded up dogies and sang to the herd at sundown?

He didn't get much horseback time that first month, but just about the time we'd wrapped up the windmill work, we had a little excitement.

It was a Sunday afternoon, "the day of rest" as they call it in the Consumer Society, and I drove over to a windmill in the middle pasture to check the water level in the tank. We had drained it and cleaned it, and we'd hit a string of still days and it wasn't filling fast enough to keep up with the cattle.

Well, after checking the tank, I noticed a Hereford cow standing off by herself in a plum thicket. That was kind of unusual, a cow standing alone in the heat of the day when most of the cattle were piled three-deep around the waterhole.

I drove over and checked her out. Two hundred feet away, I knew she was in trouble. She had a sunken look in her eyes that said she'd been in pain for several days.

The ranch had some Charolais bulls and one of them had bred this old cow and given her a bull calf she couldn't handle. I looked her over and guessed that she had been in labor for at least twenty-four hours.

The calf was long dead and the cow's nose showed that she was burning up with fever.

So much for my day of rest.

We drove back to the barn. While I caught and saddled Reno, I told Andy to gather up all our calf-pulling equipment: pulling chains, antiseptic, water, buckets, medicine, and the calf-pulling frame with the come-along built into it.

Since I didn't know what we might be getting into, I threw in extra ropes, chains, pulleys, and fence stretchers. We hooked up the gooseneck, loaded Reno, and headed north through the sandhills.

3

On the way, I told the wide-eyed Andy my strategy. If the cow would drive, I would take her back to the corrals. Since she was weak and suffering, I didn't know how long this would take or which route we would follow. It might take us two hours, and I would have to let her chose the itinerary.

If I got her started home, Andy would have to drive the pickup and trailer up a steep, washed-out trail and find his way back to headquarters.

What if the cow didn't go? "Well, you'll get in on some real cowboy work before you go back to Houston."

That excited Andy but it didn't excite me. Reno was a good pasture horse in many ways, but also high-headed and iron-jawed and otherwise poorly suited for rope jobs. And he wasn't big enough to be wallowing grown stock around.

But he was the best I had at the time.

When I approached the cow on Reno, she staked out her position right away. She greeted me with that crazy look in the eyes and that way of shaking her head that tells a guy he's fixing to earn his pay.

If I wanted her, I could ride into the plum thicket and get her. She wasn't going to the house or anywhere else without a fight.

I hollered at Andy and told him to forget about driving the pickup home. Whatever doctoring we managed to do on this old sister would be done under pasture conditions.

I took down my rope and rode in to get her. Instead, she came after me.

Old Reno had been thumped around by waspy cows, and he side-stepped her horns as she blew past us. She headed for the windmill and the trailer.

I yelled at Andy. "Stay behind the trailer until I get a rope on her. She's in a nasty mood." Andy moved behind the trailer and watched the action through the slats.

If you've ever tried to pitch a loop on a fighting cow, you know it's not an easy shot. In the first place, she's facing you and that changes all the rules about jerking slack. In the second place,

4

by the time you're within throwing range, you're also within *hooking* range.

Old Reno had figured the odds in this game and he wasn't anxious to get in too close. He danced and tossed his head while I made several sidearm throws at long range. At last, my loop dropped behind one ear. If I could ease around to the side and pull my slack, I would have her.

But at that very moment Andy's curiosity got the best of him. He stepped out from behind the trailer to get a better look. Maybe he thought I had the cow under control, but I didn't.

She wheeled around and went after him, leaving my loop in the dust. Andy's eyeballs got as big as boiled eggs when he saw those horns coming after him. He ducked around the back of the trailer, with the old cow breathing warm air on his hip pocket, and dived into the bed of the pickup.

I gave Andy a good scalding for not following orders, but it turned out to be a pretty good strategy. The old cow was so intent on figuring out how to get into the pickup with Andy that I was able to slip around behind her and stick a loop on her.

She fought the rope and I got her out into open ground, where she couldn't get me and Reno pinned against the pickup. Then I told Andy to take my second rope and try to catch her heels.

For the next fifteen minutes, I didn't know whether to laugh or cuss. Andy would creep up behind the cow with the loop in his hand, and when she looked at him, he would drop the rope and sprint to the pickup, his long hair standing straight out behind him.

He did this *six times*. I know because I counted, and cussed him every time he broke and ran. I was sorely tempted to ride up and give the old cow some room to work, but I didn't.

At last, when I'd just about exhausted my vocabulary, Andy pitched his loop, caught a heel, and held on. He tied the heel rope to the windmill tower and I stretched her out, ran for my equipment, and pulled the calf while she was standing up.

6

It was a tough delivery, and by the time I finished with her, she was ready to kill somebody. I let Andy take off the last rope.

The boy had things to learn about cowboying, but by the time he went back to Houston, he'd made a pretty good windmill hand . . . and an uncommonly good sprinter.

Bob and I

I remember the first time I met Bob's dad. It was back in the forties and I couldn't have been more than three or four years old. We lived in a big old two story house on the south edge of Perryton. The house two doors north of us was just being built.

I went exploring one day and found a nice pile of sand in front of the new house. I was in the process of building some roads on it when a man in striped overalls came out and asked me not to scatter his sand.

He had a kind way about him, so when he went back inside, I followed him. He was doing finish work on the house and I watched him. After a while I asked, "What's your name?"

"Puddin' Tane, ask me again and I'll tell you the same."

He went on about his work.

"What's your name?"

"John Brown, ask me again and I'll knock you down."

He never did tell me his name. Later I learned that it was Gordon and that he had a son named Bob. And thirty-three years later, I would pull that Puddin' Tane routine out of my memory and give it to a character in my book *Hank the Cowdog*.

I don't remember when I met Bob, but we were friends from the very beginning. He was a big strong lad for his age, had clear blue eyes and hair the color of his father's wheat at harvest time.

And he always wore the same brand of striped overalls that Gordon wore.

Bob's people on both sides of the family had come to the Panhandle when it had first opened for settlement. They had burned cow chips for fuel and suffered through bitter winters. They had farmed through the Dust Bowl and endured hardships that drove others to sell out and leave. They were sturdy folks.

Bob was sturdy too, the tallest, strongest, fastest kid in our neighborhood. Football was big with us in those days, and we knew that one day Bob would be a star with the Perryton Rangers.

He and I used to listen to the games on the radio, eating powdered donuts and drinking hot apple cider and fighting over which one was going to be Jimmy Todd. Jimmy was our star half-back and later played for TCU.

At my birthday party in October, 1951, my mother took a bunch of us boys out to Leatherman Park and turned us loose. We played football, of course. Ordinarily Bob would have been right in the middle of it, making most of the touchdowns for his team, but he wasn't feeling just right.

It was a typical autumn day in the Panhandle, with a gray sky and wind moaning in the tops of the Chinese elms. Bob stood off to himself, arms crossed for warmth, and watched. He was wearing his striped overalls and a coonskin cap.

The next day I looked for him after school and didn't find him. I went to his house and knocked on the door. Nobody was there. That evening, Mother told me that Bob was sick and his folks had taken him to Plainview.

He didn't come back the next day or the next, and then Mother told me that he had polio. I didn't know what polio meant, except that when adults spoke of it, their faces showed fear.

I wrote Bob letters and told him to get well soon, and he wrote back and said he was swimming in a special pool and having daily sessions with someone called the Ouch Man. He stayed in Plainview a long time.

I remember the day he came home. It must have been winter by then. He was wearing a coat and a little Confederate cap (we had often replayed the Civil War and had chosen the Rebel side), and he had a big grin on his face.

And I remember how shocked I was, seeing the aluminum crutches for the first time and the way he dragged himself along. This was polio, and Bob would never play for the Rangers.

You'd think that if you took a kid's legs away from him and gave him a pair of sticks to walk on, it would disrupt his life. But you know, it didn't. I got over my shock, and within a couple of hours we had adjusted to our new limitations and were scheming against them.

In time, Bob's legs grew strong enough so that he could walk without his crutches. That was a great day for both of us. He fell a lot, but I was there to give him a hand. It never occurred to us that we were handicapped or that there were things we couldn't do.

We had chickens and dogs and cats and rabbits. We went on replaying the Civil War and invented a game of walking football. When I got a chemistry set for Christmas, we went into the cat-doctor business. We put on puppet shows. We went to the farm with Bob's dad and helped him with the cattle.

One time we even risked the fires of hell. After Sunday School was over, we sneaked up to the third floor of the Baptist Church and skipped the morning preaching. We didn't know that Mr. Karber, the janitor, went through all the rooms on the third floor, checking for scoundrels, and we were caught.

We must have been in the fourth grade when we got our first exposure to Mark Twain. For months our little Panhandle town became Hannibal-on-the-Mississippi, which is a pretty good trick of the imagination.

We had a hard time finding the Mississippi on the bald prairie, but we managed. It was a drainage ditch behind the city swimming pool, and when they drained the pool every two weeks, we had our river. At high water time, we would go to the Mississippi.

A second reading of *Tom Sawyer* convinced us that, to be authentic about this business, we had to meow at night. (If you recall, Huck would slip out of the widow's house at night and call to Tom by meowing under his window.) We studied the text and memorized our parts.

I would have to be Huck on this adventure, the one who did the slipping up to the window and the meowing, because Bob couldn't do it. It had nothing to do with his legs. My bedroom was on the second story.

After dark one warm summer night, I slipped out of the house, climbed the tall white fence around Bob's back yard (could have used the gate but that wasn't in the book), and made my way through the darkness to his window.

As planned, he had left it open. I crouched down and meowed. He came to the window and said, "Is that you, Huck?" I said it was and told him to come out the window, we were going to visit the graveyard and try an incantation for smallering warts.

We didn't realized that Bob's dad had put the screens on with screws. To get out, he had to walk through the house and explain everything to his folks. We both felt pretty bad about that because it wasn't in the book.

Bob has never run since that fall day in 1951, but he walks and does what he wants. His dad died several years ago and he's running the farm now. His great grandparents are buried on the place.

I have become a writer, and *Hank the Cowdog* sure has a lot of Bob and John in it. Not long ago, I got a this letter from a fan:

"Dear Mr. Erickson: Hank the Cowdog reminds me of my own puppy, Pepper. Pepper is a miniature Schnauzer. My brother's dog, Smokey, is Pepper's best friend. Their friendship is almost just like Hank's and Drover's. I sure am glad you wrote that book, it makes me happy on gloomy days!!!!!"

It was from a girl named Melanni, Bob's nine-year-old daughter.

Calipso

Calipso was a three-year-old mare in 1979. She had a few rough edges and she came by them honestly.

On her momma's side, she came from a family of outlawed Thoroughbred race horses that never did adapt to the discipline of ranch work.

She had been a little hellion as a colt and I had lost some hide and a few clothes getting her broke to ride. She had come a long way but she was still a high-octane mare.

She certainly wasn't a pet. I knew that, but one day in April I forgot it, and I almost got some people hurt.

I had been riding her quite a bit that month in the spring roundups. She hadn't humped up with me in several weeks. One Sunday afternoon my sister, Ellen Sparks, and her two children drove up to the ranch for a visit.

The kids wanted me to take them for a ride, and I said I would. Calipso happened to be up in the corral that day and I decided to use her.

I saddled her up and rode her around the corral to warm her up and get the humps out of her back. She handled fine, but just in case she still had a hump or two that I hadn't felt, I gave my son Scot the first ride.

He was four years old and had taken a few spills, and I figured that if Calipso acted up, it wouldn't scare him as badly as the cousins from Amarillo.

I pulled Scot up behind me and we rode around the corral. We had ridden double on Calipso before and had never had any trouble. And we didn't have any trouble this time.

I gave Scot a ride and went back for Jana, my five-year-old niece. We had a good ride.

Then I went back for Erik, who was a long-legged ten-year-old. He climbed on behind me and we rode off. We had gone about fifty feet when Erik shifted his weight to find a more comfortable position and accidentally dug his heels into Calipso's flanks.

The wreck was on. My little mare bogged her head and started bucking, and in the excitement I would guess that Erik popped her again in the flanks.

We stayed aboard through several jumps and I tried to pull Calipso's head up from between her front legs.

She had a soft mouth and I must have pulled too hard, because when her head came up, the rest of her came with it. She stood straight up on her back legs and kept on coming.

Just for an instant, I thought she was going to fall over backward on top of me and Erik, but at the last second she went a little to the right and fell on her side.

Erik flew off and landed clear, and I kicked out of the stirrups and joined him in the dirt.

Neither of us was hurt, but we were lucky.

A working cowhorse is a tool, not a toy, and like any sharp tool, it can hurt someonoe when it is used improperly. The sharp edge that made Calipso a good cowhorse in the pasture made her dangerous around children.

Horses are not entirely predictable, and just about the time you think you know your favorite old saddlehorse to the marrow of his bones, he'll prove you wrong.

When you work around horses day after day, under all kinds of conditions, you become a little careless and begin taking

13

chances, trusting that the horse will behave today just as he did yesterday.

Most of the time he will, but once in a great while he'll depart from his normal pattern and do something which seems out of character.

But it's *not* out of character. It only seems that way because you have come to think of the animal as a machine or a pet.

A cowhorse is neither one. He's a very large, very strong animal whose training has made him predictable about 90 percent of the time.

An important part of being a professional cowboy lies in trying to remember, *forcing* yourself to remember, that shadowy 10 percent of the horse's mind.

The guys who forget it sometimes get their names in the paper.

Chief

In the summer of 1980 Chief was two years old. When you convert horse-years into human-years, a two-year old horse translates into an adolescent.

We had been forced to take Chief out of the horse pasture and keep him up in the corrals. He was a young stud, you see, and he had started to get interested in the wimmen.

We had three mares out in the horse pasture and all were career girls. We used them for cow work and we didn't need Chief getting them into trouble, so to speak.

So we had put him up in the corral, and there had even been some talk about how someone needed to start working with him and get him broke to ride—"one of these days when we get caught up on the ranch work."

Horse-breaking wasn't part of the work, see. It was something we did after we took care of the haying and fencing and doctoring and windmilling and mechanic work on the stock trailers.

But the weeks passed and nobody ever got around to working with the stud. He stayed around the corral, trying to find ways of making a nuisance of himself. He was pretty good at it.

He was your typical adolescent, less than a horse but more than a colt. One day he would have it in his mind that he was still a kid. He would go springing and bucking around the pen, stick his nose in the feed bucket as you walked toward the trough, and step on your toes in the process.

The next day he might be playing junior stud. He would dash around the pen and squeal at the mares out in the pasture. When they whinnied back, he would stamp his feet and snort and throw his head.

Who knows, maybe he thought he was Trigger or Secretariat, one of the big boys.

After he'd been around the corrals for a while, he developed an oral fixation. He began biting and chewing things, and one of the things he enjoyed biting and chewing was passing cowboys.

You'd be walking through the lot with your mind a thousand miles away, when suddenly Chief would strike like a cobra and get hold of a piece of your shirt. And sometimes he went deeper and got hold of living flesh.

Yes, I've read the horse manuals and I know they say that you're never supposed to slug a horse in the soft part of the nose because it's liable to make him head-shy and so forth, but I've known guys who got horse-bit and didn't stop to care what the manuals said.

And you might say that Chief got punched a few times. It didn't take him long to figure out that biting cowboys had its hazards, so then he took to chewing wood.

It's called cribbing. It's a form of neurotic behavior that some horses develop when they get bored and can't think of anything better to do. They start eating the ranch down to the ground.

Chief became a cribber. After he'd gnawed a couple of fence boards in half, he started pulling shingles off the roof of the saddle shed. It was a low roof, and before long he had stripped off the bottom three feet of shingles.

We tried to ignore this. We were awfully busy with other things, and besides, nobody on our crew was keen on jobs that couldn't be done ahorseback.

But then one night it came a big rain and my saddle and the

16

G. L. Holmes

boss's saddle were parked at the back of the shed and those one-by-four slats on the roof didn't turn much water, and the next day me and the boss rode soggy saddles.

All at once we were caught up on the ranch work. The boss held a one-man election and I got voted in as Roof Commissioner. Seems the boss had big doings in town, and Tom . . . well, Tom just melted into the sagebrush at the first mention of shingles. We didn't see him again for two days.

It was hot as blazes when I threw my bundle of cedar shingles up on the roof and went to work. Before long, I had sweat running into both eyes and one ear and down the back of my neck.

Chief came up and watched. He nipped at my boot until he got bored, and then he started pulling off my first course of new shingles.

Now, a lot of guys would have squalled and cursed and acted childish. Not me. In a calm, quiet tone of voice, I asked Chief if he'd like to wear a shingling hatchet between his eyes, 'cause if he tore off one more shingle, I was fixing to loan him mine.

Kindness works wonders. He left and I went back to work, pounding shingle nails and fingernails and talking to the sweat bees.

After a while I straightened up and throwed a couple of vertebrae back where they belonged, and I noticed it was awful quiet. I looked around for Chief.

I didn't see him, but I heard a strange noise coming from the saddle shed beneath my feet. And I noticed that somebody had left the gate open between the side lot and the saddle lot.

I jumped off the roof and trotted around to the saddle lot because I had a sneaking suspicion that somebody had also left the saddle shed door open. And if Chief was nowhere in sight, and if I had heard sounds from inside the saddle shed, and if I was the only soul on the ranch . . .

Sure nuff, he was.

I guess we'll never know why ranch animals do the things they do and go the places they go. Do you suppose I could have forced that little stud to walk into the saddle shed, if I'd wanted him in there?

No sir. I could have beat on him for a week and he wouldn't have set foot in that place, and for very good reason. He just barely fit the door, and once inside, he filled a space exactly as big as he was. If you'd slipped a shingle down both sides, you could have shimmed him between the wall and the saddle rack and he wouldn't have needed his legs to stand up.

He couldn't go forward. He couldn't turn around. He couldn't go left or right. And I didn't suppose he had brains enough to back out.

Since the shed didn't have a back door or even a back window, I couldn't get in there with him, and I wouldn't have

18

anyway because of my natural aversion to being stomped to death.

If he boogered, we could kiss the saddle shed goodbye. Also my job. I didn't figure there was a chance that I could come up with a story that would explain it. No matter how well I told it, the boss was likely to ask the identity of the guntzel son of a buck who had left a gate and a door open.

Well, when there's nothing you can do, there's no sense in worrying about it. I climbed back on the roof and went to shingling again, figuring that the pounding of my hatchet would either make things better or a lot worse.

It took Chief about half an hour to work it out in his mind that if he added three steps backward to the three steps forward that had put him in there, he'd be right back where he started— outside.

He tried it and it worked. The saddle shed was saved and so was my job. By the time the boss showed up, I had finished the shingling and swept the fresh tracks off the cement floor.

Now, you might not believe this last part, but I'll tell it anyway. That young stud never pulled another shingle off the roof, never even tried to. It could be that he learned something from the experience.

Or maybe our moving him into the back lot had something to do with it. As they say in the training manuals, "You can lead a horse to water but a pencil must be lead."

Economics

I've always heard it said that if a man was born stupid, he couldn't help it, but if he was merely ignert it was his own fault.

Now and then I get tired of being ignert. It happens about once every five years. Couple of years ago I got tired of being ignert about genetics. I didn't know a chromosome from a Crescent wrench, and in fact, I thought chromosome was a brand of Kodak film.

Many's the time I've gone into the drug store and asked for a pack of Chromosome 126. The funny part is that the film always fit the camera.

Then I took a night course on livestock genetics and learned about in-crosses and out-crosses, heterosis and halitosis, progeny testing and artificial insinuation. I learned where Charbra and Brangus and Cattalo came from and how they got their names.

I was always curious where the Cadillac and the Camelot came from, but I guess that came in the next course.

Well, that was years ago. This year I got tired of being ignert about economics. You read about it in the stock papers and the newspapers and all the magazines. Every time you turn around, there's an economist on the news or somebody's quoting an economist.

And I really didn't know what an economist was.

So I signed up for a night course in economics. Education is a wonderful thing. For thirteen weeks I read books and attended lectures and took notes. On the last night of class, I took my test and made a B, and now I have a certificate on my wall that tells the world that I know something about the science of economics.

And it is a science. It's very complicated. A man might catch on to the principles of business in a week's time because business uses common sense, but when he goes to fooling around in economics, he'll need the full thirteen weeks.

As I understand it, the science of economics is based on four basic rules. Once you get those rules down, everything else falls into place. But getting the rules down isn't easy because you have to break some old habits and start looking at things in a new way.

Anyway, here are the four rules of economics:

Economic Rule 1: *In business, the objective is to make money. In economics, the objective is to LOSE money.* (This is the part most people have trouble with at first.)

Profit slows down the circulation of money because it goes into the pockets of private citizens. Once the circulation of money is slowed, someone is liable to start counting and find out how much has disappeared.

If this news ever got out, we'd have a depression overnight. That's why politicians hire so many economists — to save us from a depression

Economic Rule 2: *When you've established yourself as a losing operation, you should begin borrowing.*

In the world of simple business transactions, money in a savings account would be considered an asset. In the world of economics, it's a liability. Not only do you have to pay taxes on productive money, but the interest you earn comes out to be less than the amount you lose to inflation.

Any economist would be suspicious of a financial statement that showed money in the bank. But a statement that showed a steady rate of loss would indicate a shrewd economic mind at work.

21

Economic Rule 3: *Keep spending, cut your income, and increase your payroll.*

On this point, there is no finer example of economic wisdom than our own federal government. Faced with the prospect of a balanced budget and troubled by a national debt of only $600 billion, government economists urged President Carter to decrease revenue by offering a tax cut, and to increase government labor costs through a public works jobs program.

That and other economic measures worked to perfection. By 1985, under the most conservative president in recent memory, we had to raise the debt ceiling to $2 trillion.

Economic Rule 4: *Continue to borrow money but also begin loaning it out at a lower rate of interest.*

This is one of the most important discoveries of modern economics. In more primitive periods of history, money was loaned out at a profit to the lender. Only in the past twenty years

have economists realized that, by borrowing money at ten percent and loaning it out interest-free, is it possible for the lender to lose ten percent *every time.*

Once again, our federal government has done pioneering work in this field, loaning vast sums money to nations that have proved time again that they have no intention of ever paying off the obligations.

These are bad loans, which means they are good, and they make the dollar weaker on the world market, which means that it's actually stronger. You get the picture.

So there is a simple lesson in economics. When you begin losing money, you can borrow. When you borrow, you can increase spending. Then you can borrow more and loan it out at a loss. The more you lose, the more you can borrow. The more you can borrow, the better your credit rating—I think.

Last week, a carnival came to town and our sheriff arrested a guy who was running a shell game—you know, guess which walnut shell has a pea under it.

I don't understand our sheriff. Maybe he never went to college. He thought the carnival guy was a crook. Shucks, I thought he was practicing Higher Economics and maybe getting ready to run for the Senate.

The Rescue

During the summer of 1970 I was working as a farmhand in the Texas Panhandle. Wheat harvest was over and it was my job to plow up 400 acres of irrigated wheat stubble.

This was back in the days before air conditioned tractors and plowing was hot, dusty, monotonous work. To pass the time, I sang over the roar of the diesel engine, memorized lines from Shakespeare, and watched whatever wildlife happened to be around, mostly jackrabbits, mice, and birds.

One morning around ten o'clock I glanced back at the tandem disc I was pulling and saw something unusual. Through the haze of dust I saw an animal jumping around in a peculiar manner.

At first I thought it was a jackrabbit, but on looking closer I saw that it was a hen pheasant. After jumping in the air several times, she landed on her back in the plowed ground and began kicking her feet.

I stopped the tractor and got down to have a closer look. When I approached her she didn't move, and I soon discovered why. She didn't have a head.

She had been sitting on a nest in the stubble, and in order to hide from me, she had stretched her neck out and flattened herself on the ground. The last disc on my plow had passed over her neck and cut off her head just as slick as though I'd done it with an axe.

Nearby I found the nest. In her thrashing she had broken three of the pastel-green eggs, and only one remained unbroken.

I was trying to support me and my wife on $400 a month, and times were tight enough so that I wasn't inclined to leave a potential Sunday dinner lying in the field.

You might say that pheasant season opened a little early that year. I dressed out the hen and, as an after-thought, slipped the one unbroken egg into my shirt pocket.

I didn't know what I would do with it, but it seemed a shame to leave it there to rot in the sun.

Two hours later I stopped for lunch. I carried my lunch box with me on the tractor, and instead of hauling the plow half a mile south to the spot where I had left the pickup, I usually ate lunch in an old abandoned farmhouse in the middle of the field.

It wasn't a terribly exciting place to spend the lunch hour, but it got me out of the sun and dust and the smell of diesel fuel. The house hadn't been lived in for 30 or 40 years. It had no glass in the windows or doors on the jambs, and its only inhabitant was a blue pigeon that lived in a small section of stovepipe that jutted out of the wall.

That pigeon and I had worked out an arrangement for sharing the house. She had possession all night and most of the day, but at noon I moved in for an hour. When she heard my boots on the old wood floor, she would fly out the south window and circle the house until I left.

And that's what she did this particular day. As I sat sprawled on the floor, gnawing a dry sandwich, I looked up at her stovepipe and wondered if she had a nest in there. I climbed up on a wooden crate and peered into the hole.

Sure enough, there was a nest with one small white egg in the center.

I wondered what Mrs. Pigeon would think if I switched eggs on her, replacing hers with one that was the wrong color and two or three times too big. She would probably push it out of the nest. But maybe not.

It was worth a try. I had already begun to suspect that I couldn't go through life with a pheasant egg in my shirt pocket.

For a couple of weeks I watched the nest. Nothing happened. The pigeon didn't push it out of the nest but it didn't hatch out either.

I had just about given up hope when, one day at noon, I climbed on the crate and peered into the hole and saw a fiesty little pheasant chick. Standing in the nest, he stared me right in the eyes, as if to say, "Yes? What is it you want?"

I was surprised and delighted that my experiment had worked. At the start I wouldn't have bet a nickle on its chances of success. Don't you know Ma Pigeon wondered what she had eaten to produce that giant green egg!

I decided to leave the chick in the nest through the afternoon and pick him up at quitting time. I would take him home and try to raise him.

About half an hour before dark, I parked the tractor for the night and returned to the old house. When I looked inside the hole, my heart sank. The nest was empty. I checked every room in the house and didn't find the chick. I had lost him.

Unlike freshly hatched pigeons and the young of most other birds, new-born pheasants are mobile at birth. They have good legs and know how to use them, and apparently this one had decided to hit the road.

That was too bad because he didn't have much chance of surviving in the wild. I had spotted some bobcat sign around the house, and I knew that bobcats were right clever at catching birds.

I was walking toward my pickup when I heard a sound. I stopped and listened. "Peep! Peep!" I didn't have any way of proving it, but I had a feeling that that was my pheasant chick. The sound came from a large area, maybe 5 acres, of tall weeds, piles of scrap lumber, and crumbling outbuildings.

The sun sat poised on the horizon. Darkness would come soon. There was no chance that I could find the chick in all that mess and it would be a complete waste of time. But I decided to try

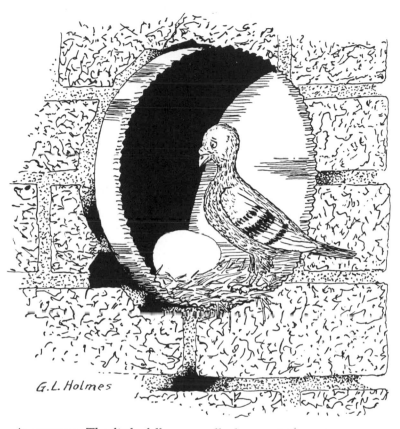

G.L. Holmes

it anyway. The little feller was all alone out there in a pretty
hostile world, and I figured he needed a friend.

I started walking toward the sound, hoping he wouldn't
stop calling when he heard me coming. I would walk a few steps,
stop and listen and get a fix on the sound, then walk some more.

Minutes passed. The sun dropped below the horizon and the
dampness of evening began to rise from the ground. I was getting
closer and the chick was still sending out his distress signal. As
long as he kept it up, he had a chance.

I dropped down to my hands and knees and started crawling
through grass and weeds that hadn't been cut or grazed in dec-

27

ades. I tried not to think about how many rattlesnakes lived around those piles of lumber and junk. I'm sure there were several, and it was strictly dumb luck that kept me from crawling into bed with one of them.

By this time it was almost dark. I knew I was getting close to the little pheasant but then he quit giving out his sound. Well, that was it. I heaved a sigh and happened to glance to my left.

There he stood in some tall weeds, staring back at me with a pair of snapping black eyes that seemed to say, "What took you so long?"

I reached out my hand, knowing he would run. But he just stood there and let me scoop him up. I dropped him into my shirt pocket, and before long we were making the twenty-mile drive back to the house. He snuggled up in my pocket and slept all the way.

If I quit the story right here, it would have a happy ending. But you've probably had enough pets around the place to know that Walt Disney didn't write the laws of nature.

The problem you have with most wild animals is that they sull up and won't eat in captivity. Rabbits are bad about that, and I never did get one raised.

But this pheasant chick moved right in and made himself at home. I don't have much respect for the intelligence of poultry, chickens in particular, but this little pheasant not only struck me as smart but also friendly. We fed him corn meal and he gobbled it up. He seemed to enjoy our company and showed no interest in running away.

When Kris was working in the kitchen, he would crawl up on her big toe and go to sleep. There for a week or so, she had to walk around with a stiff-legged limp to keep from disturbing the little prince.

The pheasant's undoing came from his friendship with our dog, Foxie. Foxie was, how shall I say this, a big, dumb, tub-footed ranch dog, the kind that never figures out where porcupine quills or skunk spray comes from.

Foxie couldn't decide how to respond to the chick. At first, when the chick came up to nuzzle at her belly, she would leap to her feet and run out of the room. My impression was that she thought the chick was giant flea, though it's hard to guess what goes on in a dog's mind.

But after a while they became friends. When we put food in the dog bowl, the pheasant would line up beside Foxie and peck away at the dog food. When Foxie took a nap, the chick would curl up in her armpit.

One Sunday afternoon they were taking a nap together. The chick was nuzzled up close to Tub-Foot, which would be about like you or me sleeping in the same bed with an elephant or a whale.

Foxie turned in her sleep and never knew that she mashed the pheasant.

We felt bad about it. We had hoped to watch the little rascal grow up. But I guess we were lucky to have him as long as we did. Any time you can get a pigeon to hatch a pheasant egg, you've beat the odds.

Foxie, The Three-Legged Dog

Foxie was one of a litter of pups our dog had in 1968. We were living in Austin at that time.

One morning around eight o'clock, I turned out Foxie and her brother, Coyote, so they could run around a little bit. Instead of staying in our yard, they dashed off to visit a dog across the street.

In the middle of the street, they were hit by a car. Coyote died at once and Foxie's right rear leg was shattered between the hip and knee. It was a compound fracture, and little pearls of bone came out the wound.

We took her to a country vet who built a splint of wire and adhesive tape. I couldn't believe the leg would ever heal, but it did. When we took off the splint, the bad leg was shorter than the good one. Foxie had acquired a permanent limp, but she could get around on it.

We never knew her breeding and didn't really care. She was a registered Soup Hound, I suppose, and just as worthless as the millions of other mutts who fall into that category.

She could eat, drink, bark at the mailman, and get pregnant. Oh, she was a terrible tramp. Even when we moved to the Mayo Ranch in Beaver County, Oklahoma, and lived miles away from

G. L. Holmes

the nearest neighbor, Foxie still managed to get herself in a family way.

I don't know how many litters of pups she brought forth, but there was a period of several years there when we were the primary source of registered Soup Hounds in Beaver County. The coyotes got a few of them, but Foxie was good mother and raised most of them to the age of weaning.

It was always interesting to watch her wean the pups, when she changed from a doting mother into a snarling witch. We would see her running on three legs across the horse pasture, with three or four pups in hot pursuit.

When she tired of running, she would turn and make her stand. Guarding her chapped nipples, she would face her brood of little parasites with lips curled around bared fangs. When one went for the milk, it got nailed. And then the yelping would begin.

Kris and I were always amused by these two sides of motherhood, and by the contrast between them. Later, when we had three children of our own, we gained some insight into Foxie's behavior.

Often we would sit around in the evening, discussing what horrible parents we had turned out to be, and we would remember old Foxie, off in the pasture, defending herself like Bowie at the Alamo against her own spawn.

Somehow it made us feel a little better, knowing that even God's innocent creatures had bad days with their children.

As a ranch dog, Foxie contributed just about what you would expect from a Soup Hound. She barked at low-flying airplanes and the swallows that nested under the eaves. She could spend an entire day running from one end of a cattleguard to the other, trying to figure out how to get a cottontail rabbit out of one of the pipes.

She never did, of course, but she never tired of trying. We figured it was cheap entertainment and, from a dog's point of view, probably more exciting than snapping at flies.

She learned about rattlesnakes by being bitten. She learned about skunks by being sprayed. She learned about coyotes by getting herself bloodied.

But then, she never really learned much, because once healed and freshened, she would do it again.

Shortly after we moved to the John Little Ranch, down on the Beaver River, Foxie jumped a porcupine. What a porcupine can do to a dog of below-average intelligence is hard to imagine unless you've seen the evidence.

When I found Foxie, she had quills in her cheeks, nose, gums, tongue, and paws; on the side of her face, around her eyes, on her forehead, and on her flanks.

No porcupine could have done all that in one shot. Foxie must have taken half a dozen swats before she figured out what a

32

porcupine does with its tail.

I fetched a pair of fencing pliers, threw a leg-lock on my poor dog, and spent an hour pulling quills.

One day when I was checking cattle on horseback, Tripod went along. She could pretty well keep up on her three legs, though she was usually a ways behind me.

We had been out an hour or so when I rode upon a half-grown badger. Fearing that it would tear Foxie apart before she figured it all out, I tried to steer her around the little brute.

But once she got the scent, there was no stopping her. She dived into the badger and the fight was on. It was a fight I didn't want. I had nothing against badgers and I figured this one was entitled to go on about his business, yet I didn't dare leave for fear he would kill my dog.

I yelled at Foxie and ordered her away, but it seemed that for both parties, this chance meeting was destined to be a fight to the death. They fought until both were exhausted, but instead of leaving at that, they lay there resting and chewing on each other, and then resumed the fight.

I didn't interfere. I couldn't. Had I gotten down, the badger might have attacked me. Had I roped the badger, he would have chewed my rope to pieces. All I could do was sit there and wait for my dog to get finished, one way or the other.

It took forty-five minutes, and it was one of the slowest, most gruesome fights I ever saw. Foxie had a 15- or 20-pound weight advantage and finally wore the badger down. Again, I tried to call her off, but she wouldn't quit until she had killed it.

People are wrong who say that man is the only animal that kills without reason. This was a senseless killing. But I figured the badger tribe would even the score if Foxie ever jumped one that was full-grown. A full-grown badger would have made hamburger out of her.

She never jumped another one, but only because she didn't find one.

As the years passed, Foxie stopped barking at birds and

chasing rabbits and getting herself pregnant by some disreputable cur. Old age set in.

Her bad leg, a small weakness in her youth, became arthritic, and the other legs, which had taken up the slack for so many years, couldn't handle the load any more.

She grew thin and cross. She slept all the time, waking only at two o'clock every afternoon to threaten the mailman. She developed sores that wouldn't heal.

I knew that I should do something to spare her from further misery and indignity. In my younger days, I wouldn't have winced at doing my duty. But at the age of forty, I found it harder to take life, no matter how miserable and hopeless.

I decided to take her to the vet and let him "put her to sleep," as we say. I always hated that euphemism and the whole idea of hiring someone to do my killing, but I just didn't have the stomach for it.

Then one evening I stepped outside the house and saw her lying under a tree. She was covered with flies that ate on her sores, as though they couldn't wait for natural death to come. Foxie would lift her head and look at them, then lie back down.

She no longer had the strength or will to protect herself from flies.

I went upstairs and got my pistol. I carried her to the pickup and laid her in the back. We went for a ride, as we'd done so many times before. I returned to town without her.

Boxing Gloves Are Cheaper Than A Broken Hand

Most of us who have worked around cattle and horses have a few stories that need some time to age and mellow. They're about things we did in haste or anger, and they weren't very funny at the time.

One of the benefits of aging is that those stories get a little less painful each year, and at some point we can even laugh about them.

I guess I'm old enough now to tell this story. It happened eleven years ago.

I had recently taken a ranch job in the Oklahoma Panhandle, and I still had a lot of foolish ideas about running my outfit just so. I wanted all my fences up in top shape and I expected my cattle to stay where they belonged.

If we were running dry cows in the middle pasture and wet cows across the fence in the west pasture, I expected those cattle to stay where they belonged because ... well, I had gone to the trouble to sort them, and by George, that's the way I wanted things to be.

Any time I found a cow in the wrong pasture, I went for a horse and moved her.

It was a matter of principle. A lot of wrecks begin as matters of principle.

Well, I was very fussy about keeping my pastures neat and orderly, so in May, when I found several stray cow calf pairs grazing in the west pasture, I went straight to the barn and saddled a horse.

The old cows were thin, and a glance across the fence told me that my neighbor was already short on grass. He had planted a field of cane for summer grazing, but it was still a long way from making a stand.

I drove the cattle north and found the place in the fence where they had gotten through. Later, I returned to the spot in the pickup and patched the hole with posts and wire.

But what makes a good fence is grass on both sides. This fence would turn a cow with a full belly, but one with hunger pains would find a hole in it. And if she couldn't find a hole, she could make one pretty quick.

For several weeks I played cat and mouse with the strays. I'd find them on my side and show up with a horse, and they would run straight to that hole in the fence. Then I would come back and cobble up another patch.

And a few days later I would find them in my pasture again.

By the first of June, I had run out of patience and was beginning to think of dirty tricks. High-life and #7 buckshot would get the attention of the cattle but not of the owner, the real culprit in the case.

I could get the owner's attention by hauling his stock to the sale barn and letting them stay there until he called the sheriff, at which time he would receive the good news that his cattle were safe and the bad news that he would have to pay the feed bill if he wanted them back.

But those were pretty drastic measures, and I wasn't quite ready to start a range war.

So, one very hot day in June, I decided on a compromise solution. I would take my toughest horse and run the strays around the pasture before letting them escape.

I figured a little exercise at a hundred degrees might make an impression on them and leave them with a few bitter memories of my side of the fence.

I saddled Reno, a half-Arabian who didn't know the meaning of tired and could run those sandhills longer and faster than a sane man cared to stay with him.

Reno and I rode out to administer the Wrath of God.

As I recall, there were three pair of thin cows with little rannihan calves at their sides. When they saw me coming, they headed straight for their favorite hole in the fence, only this time I spurred Reno and cut them off.

And for the next thirty minutes, I ran them around and around and around, from one end of the pasture to the other.

After I'd run off two months' worth of tallow and had their tongues hanging down around their front hooves, I shoved them up to the fence and let them go. They lined up like trained dogs and hopped over.

All but one calf, that is. There's always one that can't find the gate, and couldn't find it if you tore out half a mile of fence and drew him a map.

His momma had taken him through that hole in the fence so many times that the ground on both sides was smoother than the county road in front of my house, but still he couldn't find it.

Stupidity of that magnitude would be unbelievable if it weren't so common.

The little dunce bounced off the fence three or four times and blatted for his mommie. Then he came off the wires and high-balled it toward the other end of the world.

That was something I hadn't expected. I wouldn't have cared if his old lady had died of heat stroke, but separating a calf from it's mother, in a country full of veal-loving coyotes . . . that sort of went against the Cowboy Code.

I was hot and tired and dripping sweat and feeling the sting of a fresh set of galls on my legs. I had every reason to let that little stupe go and find the fate he deserved, but I just couldn't bring myself to be that cold-blooded.

37

G. L. Holmes

So I took down my rope and went after him.

There was a time in my cowboy career when I became a pretty salty pasture roper and could handle my slack well enough to zip up a loop on a squirmy little calf. Unfortunately, that moment lay some three years in the future.

A good pasture roper is a guy who's fool enough to get himself into a jam but skilled enough to get out. In 1974 I knew just enough about a rope to get myself into trouble, then to back off and get into a whole lot more.

I took after the calf, whipping and spurring and swinging that invention of the Devil, the simple twine that can hang you more ways than you have fingers and toes to count.

I don't suppose that calf had gotten more than two cups of milk out of his momma in his whole life, and I'll never know where he got his energy, but he ran like a greyhound, dodged like a goat, and didn't have enough flesh on him to stop a good loop.

I threw and I threw and I missed and I howled and I cursed — myself and the dadgum rope and Reno and, most of all, the little snot-nosed calf that was taking my dignity apart, loop by loop.

Don't expect an honest report on how many loops I spilled. In our country, the meter shuts off at five.

I missed five loops, and finally on #6, I slopped it on. By that time, I'd seen half the ranch go by and had checked the water and salt at five windmills.

And I was *so mad*, so utterly humiliated, so disgusted at my sorry display of roping that I was ready to put some veal cutlets into the deep freeze.

I threw a half-hitch over my dallies, yanked a pigging string off the back of the saddle, and stormed down the rope, grabbed an ear in one hand and flank skin in the other, rolled the calf up on my knees, and threw him to the ground as hard as I could.

He bounced up before I could catch his front leg, and I had to do it all over again. This time I rammed my knee into his flank and he bounced no more. I slipped the noose of the pigging string over his front hock, gathered up the hind legs, and started to wrap.

Somehow he kicked out, and with one of those sharp little back hooves, he rolled up about six inches of skin on the inside of my forearm.

That was too much. I couldn't stand it any more. Half-blinded by sweat and half-crazy with frustration, I drew back my right fist and aimed a punch at the fleshy part of his neck.

That might have worked, if he hadn't moved just then. But he did, and instead of hitting the fleshy part of his neck, my fist slammed into the hardest, thickest part of his skull, the area right between his horns.

I'd like to say that he quivered, straightened out his legs, and died within minutes, but that ain't the way it went. He didn't even know he'd been hit, but I sure as heck did because something snapped inside my hand.

And when I went to finish my wraps, it didn't act just right.

By the time I made it back to the barn, the old hand had puffed up and started pounding. But I couldn't quit. I still had a calf tied down out there in the pasture, and he'd die in the heat if I didn't do something with him.

I tied the hand in a rag, hooked up the gooseneck, and spent the next hour hauling the neighbor's rannihan calf back to its fence-busting mother — and cussing myself all the way.

By the time I made it in to Doc Harvey's office in Beaver, there wasn't much mystery about what I'd done. Doc looked at my swollen paw and said, "Yep, you busted her up pretty good. How'd you do it?"

You just don't lie to the doctor who's splinting your broken bone. I told him the whole story and he chuckled all the way through the making of the plaster cast. I think it made his day a little brighter.

Maybe he knew that as long as this world can match up a stupid calf with a stupid cowboy, the doctors won't have to advertise for business.

Christmas In The Panhandle

During the winter of 1979 I worked as a cowboy on the LZ Ranch south of Perryton. I remember one bitter day in December when Tom Ellzey and I were loading snow-covered bales of alfalfa hay onto the flat-bed pickup.

We wore our chaps and wool long-johns. Our fingers and toes were numb with cold, our noses and cheeks red. Our breath hung as fog in the air. We were chewing tobacco and singing the "For Unto Us A Child Is Born" chorus from Handel's "Messiah," I taking the tenor part and Tom the bass.

And aside from the grunting and spitting, it wasn't too bad. Handel might have disowned it, but Tom and I didn't care. We figured there weren't too many ranch cowboys in the Panhandle who could out-sing us on the "Messiah."

It was the Christmas season and the Perryton Community Chorus had begun rehearsing "Messiah." Tom and I had sung with the chorus for many years, long enough so that we knew most of our parts by memory.

This year, if the performance didn't get snowed out, we would have a string ensemble coming from the Amarillo Symphony and a couple of hired soloists from West Texas State. It was all directed—strings, soloists, pipe organ, and a chorus of eighty

Perryton singers—by a local rancher: my boss and Tom's dad, Lawrence Ellzey.

The weather was lousy but we didn't get snowed out. During the performance, while Lawrence sang the baritone solo, "Darkness Shall Cover The Earth," I caught myself thinking that here was a remarkable man, one whose gifts had touched me and the entire community. He had started this Perryton tradition of singing the "Messiah" 25 years ago, back during the drought of the 50s when he was going broke in the cattle business.

He was 69 years old. I had heard him use that big resonant baritone to curse cattle and ornery horses. Now it rose to the vaulted ceiling and filled every corner of the Methodist Church. I couldn't imagine that it had ever been better, even in his youth. It sent chills down my back.

Cowboying and singing the "Messiah:" that's an odd combination, isn't it? Yet some of my most pleasant memories of Christmas in Perryton contain both. To most people, the very suggestion that you might find a couple of Panhandle cowboys singing "For Unto Us A Child Is Born" on top of a haystack would bring smiles of disbelief. If you tried to write that into a novel, it would never work.

One of the nice things about being a small town author is that you not only observe life, but you participate in it. You become aware of the paradoxes in human experience. You see heroism in quiet moments and find transcendence in odd places.

That's not a bad thing to remember at Christmas, for surely one of the great paradoxes of all time is that the inspiration for Handel's majestic oratorio was a child born two thousand years ago—in a hay manger.

Our Congressmen Need
Our Donations

It was one of those lovely Panhandle days, with a forty mile an hour wind out of the north and the sky full of Kansas real estate.

Around noon, a lady was crossing Main Street and got hit by a tumbleweed. It drug her two blocks before they could get her loose and take her to the hospital.

This was back in 1977, as I recall, and I had taken the day off to drive into town and attend the livestock auction. It's fun to leave the ranch once in a while and go to the sale. I spent my month's profit on a piece of custard pie, wandered into the sale barn, and sat down beside a character named Bloodhound McGee.

People call him Bloodhound because he's always got a sad hound dog look on his face. He's an older gentleman, probably about sixty, and you can recognize him a block away because of the way he walks, all humped over like he's got a tombstone tied to his back.

They say Bloodhound went into farming two weeks before the Dust Bowl. He starved out but came back and bought himself a little place just in time for the drought of the fifties. He jumped into the cattle business in 1973, when everybody was making

43

money, and the very next day the cattle market started for the bottom.

In 1964 he joined the Real Gospel Church, and it was that spring that a tornado came through and blew it away. Several years ago, he gave to the Heart Fund, and that very night the chairman of the drive died of a coronary.

Last year, he tried to make a donation to the Cancer Society, but the committee voted to refund his money with interest.

He's had hard luck. I guess he deserves to look like a bloodhound.

Anyway, I sat down beside him at the sale. "How's everything out your way, Bloodhound?"

His big, sad eyes came up. "Oh, not so bad. Wheat's dead. Field's blowing away. Got greenbugs in the bindweed. Out of grass, out of feed, had to bring a cow into the sale." He glanced toward the sale ring. "Here she comes now."

I leaned forward and squinted my eyes. For a minute there, I thought that was the biggest greyhound I'd ever seen. But then I saw the tag in her ear and knew it was a cow.

It took three grown men to get her into the ring. The auctioneer put her in at a dollar a hundred, and the bidding went down from there. She sold for fifty cents a hundred and weighed seven hundred.

After they took out commission and yardarge, Bloodhound got a check for a dime.

"Well," he sighed, "I guess I can buy a cup of coffee."

I didn't have the heart to tell him that coffee had just gone up to a quarter. "What have you been feeding that cow?"

"Gunny sacks and broomweed. I run 'em through the grinder and add salt to hold down consumption."

"I don't think it worked, Bloodhound. Looks to me like she's had consumption for several months."

He bobbed his head up and down. "She looks pore, all right. I'm just glad I didn't bring any of the thin cows to town, bad as this market is."

44

"You mean you've got cows thinner than that one?"

"Yalp. Having to feed 'em extra. Throwed 'em out some fence posts with good bark this morning."

"Times are tough, Bloodhound."

He turned clear around in his seat and stared at me. "Times are tough around here, but they must not be so bad in Washington. Them politicians just voted themselves a pay-raise of $13,000. Do you realize how many cows I'd have to sell in a year to make what they voted themselves in five minutes?"

I turned a sale bill over and did some figgering. "Looks like ... let's see here, naught naught carry your one, a hundred and thirty thousand head of cows."

"That's right. A hundred and thirty thousand head of cows to make—not their whole salary, but just the raise they voted themselves this year. And that ain't counting the raise they got last year, or their pension or their travel expense or their office allowance."

I shrugged. "Well, what else can we do, Bloodhound? If we don't give our congressmen a decent wage, politics will become a rich man's profession."

His eyes widened. "I got news for you, boy. Any son of a gun who can get a raise of $13,000 a year IS a rich man."

"Not really. They have a lot of expenses you and me don't have. They have to keep up two homes."

"Uh huh. One for the old lady and one for the chippies."

"They have to send their children to private schools."

"To get around bussing, which they voted for."

"And they have to entertain a lot."

"Gettin' drunk, we call it."

"And they have to travel back to the home district . . ."

"And to Aspen and Switzerland."

". . . to see what the voters think about the issues."

"Issues! The only issue in Washington is whether to spend more or *much* more. That's something a monkey could decide for two bananas an hour."

"Bloodhound, congressional salaries have to be close to what they could get in business and industry."

He brought his face closer to mine. "How much do you think a business would pay a man who couldn't balance the company budget and managed to lose a hundred billion a year?"

"Hmmm."

"I'd let him sweep out and pay him fifty dollars a week. What would you do?"

"Well, you've got a point, Bloodhound."

"The only good thing about the whole deal is that they've tied this pay raise to a new code of essex."

"I think it's 'ethics.' "

"Whatever, but I think that part's all right." He stuck a finger in his ear and drilled out some wax. "If we can buy honest politicians for only $13,000 a year, we'd better do it before they raise the price."

"Good point."

All at once he sat up straight and looked at a cow in the ring. "Hey, somebody's selling one of my cows."

Sure enough, I saw Bloodhound's brand right there on top of her ribs. "You reckon somebody stole her?"

"Yalp."

"You going to call the sheriff?"

He fell back into his usual slouch. "Nope. If a little extra money can reform a politician, it might make an honest man out of a cow thief. Anyway, what else can you buy for a dime?"

Quicksand

When I went to work on the Beaver River in the spring of 1978, I didn't know much about quicksand, since I had spent the last four years cowboying on a sandhill ranch that didn't even have a spring of live water, much less a bog hole.

One afternoon, around the first of June, my boss told me that one or more of our cows had strayed from the west meadow pasture into Leland Barby's Duck Pond Creek pasture. He wanted me to ride over there and see what I could find.

I saddled up Little John and headed south from headquarters. I crossed the river at a shallow spot and rode toward a gate in the southwest corner.

I left the gate down and went on into the Duck Pond pasture. I didn't find any cattle on the north end, so I rode on to the south end. I found all the cattle there, watering at some spring pools on Duck Pond Creek.

This pasture was leased out to Bobby and Elven Gregg of Beaver, who were running yearling steers on it for the summer. I found two LD Bar cows among the steers and tried to cut them off. But I had some trouble. Five Gregg steers had become attached to the cows, as steers will do, and I couldn't separate them. So I decided to drive them all to the gate and try to cut off the steers on the way.

I drove them north, threw them onto the fence, and headed them toward the gate. I rode in and cut off the steers, but they just ran in a circle and came back to the cows. I worked Little John as hard as I dared, since the afternood was quite warm, and finally gave up. Two riders might have cut off the steers, but I wasn't able to do it by myself.

I ended up putting all of them into the west meadow. I shut the gate and walked Little John toward home. He was hot and dripping sweat.

When we came to the river, I walked him out into the middle and let him drink. Since he was so hot, I decided to ride him down the stream so that the water could cool his feet, which is the quickest way of cooling a horse down. The river was shallow at this point, only about a foot deep, and I couldn't see anything wrong with riding down the middle of it.

We had gone about fifty feet when the trap door opened up. Little John's front end went down in quicksand and I flew over his head and landed in the river. My reactions were good. I kicked free fo the stirrups and hit the water rolling to get away from his front hooves.

When I pulled myself out of the water, I saw that Little John had buried his left front leg up to the shoulder. He thrashed and struggled to get out but he didn't make any progress. When he had exhausted himself, he just rolled over and gave up, and his nose went under the water. I had the reins in my hands and lifted his head out of the water.

I was shocked when his head went under. He just seemed to give up the fight. It's hard for me to believe that he would have drowned if I hadn't been there, but maybe he would have. This was the first time I had ever bogged a horse badly in quicksand, so I didn't know what to expect. I held his head up for three or four minutes, while he lay there panting and blinking his eyes.

By this time, I was doing some fast thinking. What did a man do about a horse that was high-centered in the river? I was alone and half a mile from headquarters. If I went back to the

49

G. L. Holmes

house, Little John might drown by the time I got back with a pickup and shovel. But if I stayed there, about all I could do was hold his head out of the water.

And there was one more problem: The saddle on his back belonged to *me*, and it was getting soaked. I wasn't making enough money in this job to buy a new $900 saddle. If I couldn't save the horse, I might have to cut the cinches and save the saddle.

I gave Little John time to rest and catch his wind, and then I started pulling his head around in the direction his feet were pointing. He didn't respond.

I pulled on the reins and yelled at him. He stiffened his neck and started struggling again, and at last he wallowed to his feet.

50

I led him straight to the north bank. He was out of breath and dripping water and quivering, and I was in a similar condition. Both my boots were filled with water, I was soaked from top to bottom, and I could feel sand on the inside of my pants. But we were both alive, and after a short rest, we headed back to the barn.

From that moment on, I began treating the Beaver River with respect, and I started asking questions and learning more about quicksand. I discovered that the river was most likely to be boggy in the spring, after a big rise. When the river "rolls," the sand in the stream bed is disturbed and mixed with water. During the summer months or during a dry spell, the water seeps out and the sand settles, becoming less "quicky."

One old cowboy who worked on the river for many years told me that he never put a horse into the river until he found a place where cattle or deer had crossed first. I thought that was pretty good advice and I followed it whenever I could. I also made it a practice to pull my feet out of the stirrups when I had to cross, so that if my horse went down, I wouldn't get a leg pinned beneath him.

One day I was talking to Hobart Hall, a long-time cowboy on the Open A Ranch, and I asked him about quicksand. He said that one winter he was crossing the river when the water was chest-deep on a horse. He and another man had gone over to the south side to check some heifers and were on their way back to headquarters.

Out in the middle of the river, Hobart's horse got into some quicksand and went down. Hobart cleared the saddle and went into the water, thinking that he had better get on the downstream side of the horse and stay clear of his thrashing front feet. But the horse caught him with his hooves, pushed him under water, *pinned him on the bottom, and stood on him.*

Lucky for him, his partner saw what had happened and came to his rescue, saving the Open A the expense of a cowboy funeral.

Another time, Hobart bogged a paint horse in quicksand.

51

The paint got so mad that every time Hobart came close, the horse tried to bite him. The horse finally got out, but from then on, he wouldn't go into the river unless another horse had crossed first, and no amount of whipping and spurring would change his mind.

Hobart believed that some horses bogged down worse than others, and that the difference lay in the way they moved. He said that Ralph Barby, his boss on the Open A, used to ride a horse that never went down in quicksand, even when horses around him did. He moved with short, rapid steps when he crossed a river, and Hobart thought this is what kept him from bogging down.

I heard many tales about quicksand after that, and I heard several cowboys claim that the Cimarron was more treacherous than the Beaver. I worked on the LD Bar for fifteen months and crossed the river hundreds of times. I never got into quicksand again and was never with anyone else who did.

But I didn't forget my first experience with quicksand—or forget Hobart Hall's story about lying underwater with a horse standing on top of him.

Rocks Are Charming

We went to Kerrville last summer and stayed for a couple of weeks on a ranch.

The Hill Country is just about everyone's favorite part of Texas, and I can see why. The place has a lot of charm, and much of what is charming is made out of rock.

I never saw so many rocks. My first reaction to the Hill Country was conditioned by my years as a Panhandle cowboy: "Where is the dirt? Don't they have any *dirt* around here? How can grass grow if there isn't any *DIRT*? What do cattle eat in Kerr County?"

The answer is that there aren't many cattle in Kerr County, just goats and high-powered horses. Goats will eat almost anything and horses eat profit. Both do well around Kerrville. I can't remember whether cattle have four or five stomachs, but to thrive in this area they would need thirteen.

The major livestock species in the Hill Country isn't cattle or goats or horses. It's deer.

Hill Country ranchers have managed to turn a staggering disadvantage—no dirt, too many hills, way yonder too many rocks—into a source of income. They have found what is probably the perfect way to ranch in a consumer society.

Instead of struggling to raise beef cattle, which are almost sure to break your heart, your health, and your pocketbook, they raise deer — which would be here whether ranchers had decided to raise them or not.

Deer raise themselves on rocky cedar-covered hills that are beautiful only to deer and humans outside of agriculture. Deer don't have to be gathered or worked, branded, vaccinated, loaded, prayed over or cried over.

But here's the best part: deer are harvested by the consumers, the guys from Dallas and Houston who come out in the fall to shoot them — not for wages, not even for free. They *pay* for the privilege, and they pay a lot.

By the time you figure in the deer lease, wardrobe, artillery and ordinance, cutting and wrapping, and motel rooms, deer figures to be the most expensive meat in the modern world. If you include the liquor bill, it becomes the most extravagant dish in all recorded history.

If you tried to sell venison in the supermarket, there would be no consumer revolt, only laughter. Who needs venison at $45 a pound when you can get chicken gizzards for a buck twenty-nine?

Hill Country ranchers have a good thing going for them. To accomplish the same thing in the Panhandle, we would have to sell Mexican sandburs for $50 a bushel, range delivery. It will never happen.

Our five-year-old daughter, poor Panhandle child, had never seen a deer before we went to Kerrville. We had to explain things to her: "That is a doe, which is a momma deer. The baby is called a fawn and the daddy is called a buck."

"A duck?"

"A *buck*. And that thing over there in the trees is called a deer blind."

Ashley thought about this for nine days, and then she asked, "Daddy, why are deer blind?" I had never thought about that.

Another thing that impresses a visitor from the Panhandle is the abundance of water around Kerrville. It's everywhere, it's clear, it's stunning in its beauty.

54

G. L. Holmes

Maybe you have to be from a dry country to appreciate something like the Guadalupe River. If we had one of those in the Panhandle, we would have to build a cyclone fence around it to keep people from trying to steal it.

It is such a friendly river, compared to our Canadian. The Canadian has no pecan trees or cypress trees, no waterfalls, no emerald pools. It offers jungles of scrubby salt cedar, deer flies, cockleburs, and six-to-ten inches of gyp water flowing over quicksand.

The Guadalupe beckons you to come and stay. The Canadian beckons you to pass by and keep going.

The Guadalupe's water is clear because it flows over a bed of stone, and because the country it drains has so little topsoil. That brings us back to rocks. Rocks make pretty rivers. In our day, people will pay almost any price to own a stretch of pretty water.

Around Kerrville, rocky land with running water will bring $5,000 an acre or more. This same land would starve an onion or a radish to death, but it looks pretty and people are paying for pretty country.

What stumps me about the Hill Country is how it can support such magnificent trees: sycamores, oaks, pecans, walnuts, cypress. They seem to grow out of solid bedrock.

I know people in the Panhandle who plant trees in good rich soil, water them every day, fertilize them regularly, and fuss over them for years, as though they were the last of a dying species.

And yet for all their labor, they can't begin to duplicate what Nature has done in the Hill Country with haphazard seeding and poor planning.

Those gorgeous pecans along the Guadalupe almost bring tears to a plainsman's eyes. We would give almost anything to have just *one* of those trees in Perryton. We would give it the keys to the city, make it honorary mayor, guard it twenty-four hours a day.

We could offer it love, affection, respect, and devotion, as well as twenty-seven inches of the richest topsoil in Texas. Yet those stupid trees have chosen to live in Kerr County—among rocks. How can Nature do so well with such poor management?

One afternoon in August, I took the family on a scenic drive, from Kerrville to Harper, then over to Ingram and down the Guadalupe to Kerrville again. I wanted the kids to soak up some of the Hill Country charm before we took them back to face another Panhandle winter.

Scot, our nine-year-old, has never been one to burst into poetry about anything. He is your archetypal boy, made of snails and rails and puppydog tails. He is drawn to things that make noise: trucks, bulldozers, helicopters, laser pistols, and a little sister who will squeal if poked often enough.

On the scenic drive, I urged Scot to *look*—to observe, see, feel, and soak up the countryside. As we neared the outskirts of Ingram and crossed a lovely wooded creek, Scot finally yielded to the Hill Country charm and composed a poem. Let's see if I can remember it:

> "See this finger?
> See this nose?
> See this booger?
> Here it goes!"

Well, so much for charm. But all was not lost. Scot gathered up fifty pounds of rocks and took them home.

Show Biz Government

A lot of the guys at the feed store claim that our Department of Energy doesn't do anything.

"Here we are in an energy crisis," they say, "and we've got a Department of Energy that spends $12 billion a year and has yet to find one quart of oil or dig one bushel of coal out of the ground."

I used to think the DOE didn't do anything either, but now I know better. I was driving back to headquarters yesterday afternoon in the four-wheel drive. I had just dropped off fifteen bales of moldy hay for the cows in the middle pasture.

I had the radio on and I heard this new song come over the air. I didn't catch all the words, but it started off with, "Everybody's doing it," sung by a torchy female vocalist who was backed up by a pounding disco beat.

These days, songs about somebody "doing it" are as common as cornbread, and ordinarily I don't pay much attention to them. But this woman was raising such a fuss that I listened.

And I made an interesting discovery. What everybody is "doing" ain't what you and I thought they were "doing." What they are "doing" is driving fifty-five miles an hour—to save energy!

"Brought to you as a public service by the United States Department of Energy."

So much for the boys down at the feed store who criticize the Department of Energy. The DOE may not be out drilling for oil or digging for coal, but by George they're sure writing foxy little songs and getting them on the radio.

Okay, maybe $12 billion is a little stout, but we can't expect to get Show Biz Government for nothing. It takes a lot of people and a lot of salaries and a lot of pensions to get good advice on the radio.

You know, there's quite a lot of Show Biz Government on the radio nowadays. Some of the spots, like the one from DOE, offer catchy tunes. Others feature little animals who talk. There's Smokey the Bear and Woodsie the Owl and McGruff the Crime Dog.

Smokey urges us not to burn our country down, which is a pretty good idea. Woodsie wants us to give a hoot so we won't pollute, another good idea, and it also rhymes. And McGruff has come up with a solution to crime: shift the responsibility for crime to law-abiding citizens. I wouldn't have thought of that myself.

The federal agencies that produce these public service messages use songs and jingles and little animals to get their points across because, well, they want to help us and they know we're not very smart. And they're dealing with some pretty deep, heavy-duty stuff.

You take the one about children's toys. I don't remember who put it out, the Products Safety Commission or some such outfit, but their message was very important. In fact, you might want to write this down and tape it to the ice box door:

"CHILDREN SHOULD NOT SWALLOW TOYS!"

That toy bulldozer might appear innocent, but let a kid swaller it and there's no telling what might happen. Parents should be warned against letting their kids swaller toy bulldozers and tractors and electric trains and even tennis balls and stuff like that. And here's another one:

"TOYS WITH SHARP EDGES CAN CUT, AND TOYS WITH ROUGH EDGES CAN BRUISE, AND TOYS WITH FAULTY WIRING CAN SHOCK!"

So there you are. Boy, you've got to be careful with toys.

That same agency did a piece about how to buy a bicycle. According to their research, you should go to a bicycle shop to shop for a bicycle. Bicycles come in different sizes, so you should try to buy the correct size.

That's pretty crucial, buying the correct size bicycle.

Then there's the one they did on how to buy a Christmas tree, which pointed out that if you have a little room, you probably should buy a little tree. Oh, and the most important thing to remember is not to burn your house down at Christmastime because that would be very sad.

But you think Christmas is dangerous? It's nothing compared to Halloween. After listening to all the warnings on the radio this year, we decided to quit buying candy and costumes and punkins, and we locked the kids in the front closet until the second week in November.

Did you hear the one on how to buy a used car? Shop around, compare prices, and don't make any dumb decisions.

And household chemicals? Some household chemicals aren't good for you. You should always read the label before you drink Liquid Plumber.

About a year ago, the Texas Attorney General's office got into Show Biz Government. They had a big radio campaign to protect consumers against bill collectors (I liked that one) and others to protect consumers from hustlers and crooks.

It was kind of an odd coincidence that our attorney general was under indictment at that time. Some of the boys at the feed store thought maybe he was buying votes with state money, but I said, "Surely not. How dumb does he think we are?"

The President's Council on Physical Fitness did one a couple of years ago. According to them, children need exercise, and they had a free booklet for parents who didn't know about exercise.

G.L. Holmes

They've got a lot of free booklets that you can get from the Consumer Information Service in Pueblo, Colorado. "How To Boil An Egg Without Burning Yourself." "How To Open A Can Of Beans Without Losing A Finger." "How To Flush The Toilet Without Falling In." Things you can use every day.

The Department of Agriculture did a commercial not so long ago that brought Show Biz Government pretty close to home. It revealed that accidents can and do happen on the farm. Not only can a guy get himself run over by his own tractor, but he can slip on fresh manure.

Unfortunately, they didn't have anything to say about the guy who gets run over by the federal government, but I'll give them one thing. They're the world's leading experts on manure.

Stampede!

One of the big differences between cowboying today and cowboying a hundred years ago is that modern cowboys don't have much call to be ahorseback after dark.

That always suited me just fine. I never had the slightest desire to handle cattle at night, and in eight years of full-time cowboy work, I only had to do it once.

It was about this time of year, November of 1979. I was working for Tom and Lawrence Ellzey on their Wolf Creek ranch, 25 miles south of Perryton.

The day started out like any other, with a list of things to do about as long as your arm and only ten hours of daylight to do it in. Lawrence had found a buyer for 124 head of heavy yearling steers we had summered on grass, and our main job for the day was for me and Tom to round up the north pastures, sort and shape a selling herd of 700-800 pound steers, and then drive them two miles south to the home pasture.

But before we could get to that job, we had to feed and doctor 20 light steers in the sick pen, and feed hay to a bunch of steers we were weaning in the side lot.

This was a busy time of year because we hadn't yet shipped the big steers and we were already receiving fresh cattle for winter grazing on wheat pasture. We had cattle stuck everywhere, in every pasture, trap, and pen on the ranch, and they all had to be tended to.

After we'd fed and doctored the steers in the corral, we saddled two horses, gathered 155 light steers in the home pasture, and drove them over to the alfalfa field.

Tom had done some investigating and had learned that we could pasture the green alfalfa, which was a bit of a surprise since we had always heard that green alfalfa was too rich for cattle and would cause them to bloat and die.

But Tom had discovered that alfalfa is most toxic at night, and that cattle could eat it during the warm part of the day without much danger. That meant we had to turn the steers into the alfalfa patch around ten in the morning and drive them off around sundown.

It was noon before we got all the little jobs done around headquarters. We ate a quick lunch, loaded our horses in the stock trailer, and drove three miles north to an old hogwire pen called the Four Corners Corral.

We got ahorseback, gathered the big steers out of the northwest pasture, penned them, and then gathered the rest of the shipping steers out of the northeast pasture. We did some sorting in the corral, cutting off a few steers that didn't quite fit the bunch, then opened the gates and started driving them south across country to the home pasture.

These old steers had been driven before, and they strung out in a long line and drove nicely. Tom rode the point and I stayed back on the drag. It was a beautiful fall afternoon: still, golden, just warm enough for a man to be comfortable in a long-sleeve flannel shirt.

The only problem we encountered on the drive came about a mile outside the pens, when a small group of light steers that were located in the middle pasture got mixed in with our herd. There were four of them. We drove three out of the herd, and when the fourth wouldn't leave, we roped him and dragged him out.

64

It was four o'clock by the time we pushed the steers into the home pasture. The shadows were growing long and, as so often happened, we were racing the sun again. We still had half a day's work left to do, and only two hours of daylight.

Since we had located the shipping steers in the home pasture, we had no place to go with the light steers that were on the alfalfa. We *had* to get them off that green alfalfa for the night or they would start bloating and dying on us.

We loped our horses back to headquarters, loaded up fencing equipment in the pickup, raced over to the alfalfa field, and started building a temporary electric fence around a little piece of grass in the southwest corner of the field.

We could hold the steers in the temporary trap for the night. That would keep them away from the green alfalfa while it was in its toxic state.

While Tom set the corner posts with a sixteen-pound sledge hammer, Lawrence and I strung the wire and set the line posts. By this time, the sun had gone down and we were running from post to post to get the job finished.

Using the headlights of Lawrence's pickup, we wired up the fence to the electric charger and tested it. It worked! We had ourselves a temporary pasture. Now all we had to do was round-up 155 head of silly steers and push them into the trap—in the dark.

Tom and I jumped into his pickup and drove back to headquarters, found our horses in the dark corral, tightened our cinches, and rode back to the alfalfa field on Happy and Calipso.

The temperature had fallen to 35 degrees and there was no moon. We trotted our horses toward the headlights of Lawrence's pickup, over broken country, up and down ravines, and hoped that our horses could see better than we could. What we could see was exactly nothing. I couldn't see Tom, he couldn't see me, and neither of us could see the ears of our horses.

"This is liable to get western," I said.

"Sure might," came Tom's reply.

Lawrence had figured out that we wouldn't be able to find the gate into the field, so he had driven his pickup to the gate and shined his headlights on it. We went through the gate and started rounding up cattle.

This was a new experience for both of us, and I'll never forget the eerie feeling I got gathering cattle in total darkness. We could *hear* them but we couldn't see them. We couldn't see the fences, we couldn't judge distances. We tried to rely on our memory of the terrain, but we quickly lost all sense of direction.

All we could do was go by sound and push everything toward the lights of Lawrence's pickup.

At one point, I had been following a sound for quite a distance when Lawrence swung his pickup around and in the brief flash of his headlights, I saw that I had been rounding up Tom's dog.

At last we cleared the field and had all the steers down at the southwest corner. Lawrence shined his lights on the gate and we began easing the steers into the trap. This was like handling rotten eggs. We knew that any sudden movement or noise from us could start a stampede.

They funneled through the gate, very slowly. We had pushed them all through the gate and had begun to relax and think about pulling off our boots in front of a warm fire, when they boogered.

We never knew what it was that set them off. Maybe it was the dog. Maybe it was the snap of a weed. Maybe it was nothing but typical bovine stupidity, but all at once the wreck was on.

I had read the memoirs of old traildrivers who told hair-raising stories of cattle stampeding in the night, of cowboys spurring their horses through inky darkness to turn the lead steers, of horses cartwheeling to the ground and cowboys getting broken and trampled.

I had enjoyed reading those stories, but I had never felt any urge to try it myself. But here it was. We couldn't see the stampede, but we could hear the rumble of hooves and the snapping of brush.

We spurred our horses into a gallop and plunged through the darkness, riding toward what our ears told us was the front of the herd. We slapped our leggings and yelled. We had to stop them before they hit the fence.

But there was no stopping them. Off to my right, I heard the twang of the wire, followed by Tom shouting curses. The steers had just wiped out the fence we had worked so hard to build for them. It had taken us three hours to build it and them only thirty seconds to lay it flat on the ground.

We were cold, hungry, disgusted, and tired to the bone, but we couldn't quit. Lawrence drove up in the pickup and we made plans while the horses caught their wind.

We had only one option left—cut the fence on the east and drive the steers out into a plowed field. They would have nothing to eat and by morning they might be scattered all over the Wolf Creek valley, but that was the best we could do.

So with Lawrence and his headlights in the middle and a cowboy on each side, we made another sweep through the field. Lucky for us, they didn't stampede again and we got them off the alfalfa before they could eat any more of it.

I got home that night around ten o'clock, and when I finally pulled off my boots, I knew I'd put in a day's work.

Tax Reform

The days grow longer. A soft wind caresses the tulips and carries the scent of greening grass.

The sky changes. The stark flat clouds of winter yield to puffy thunderheads that promise rain. The ice of last December slips into memory.

Throughout the centuries, mankind has responded with song and poetry to the changing of the seasons. Ancient man celebrated the coming of spring and saw it as a rebirth of nature.

Life was good, life had returned!

It has only been in recent years that mankind in certain quarters of the globe has greeted the coming of spring with increased consumption of antacids and tranquilizers, and has begun to wonder if the rebirth of life is such a good idea.

For in America, winter is not followed by spring. It is followed by INCOME TAX.

Putting Tax Day in the spring of the year was a bad idea. The symbolism that has grown up around income tax, which dwells on fear, depression, anger, and frustration, simply doesn't belong in a period of growth and fecundity.

If we must have this tax, then we should move it into its proper season — say, December 15 when there is already a certain brooding atmosphere upon the land.

68

That would give us the entire spring to recover, and fools that we are, by March we would probably be singing and laughing again, just as though we were not waltzing toward another tax deadline.

But the maddening thing about our tax system is that it mocks our efforts to improve it. Every time we "reform" it, we make it worse. Every balanced budget turns into a deficit, every tax cut increases our taxes, every effort to make the forms comprehensible makes them more incomprehensible.

Hence, even if we moved Tax Day into the dreariest part of the year, where it belongs, we could expect the usual result of tax reform: things would get worse.

For one thing, there's the suicide problem to consider. A group in New England has been studying suicides in the United States and has noted (to no one's surprise, I would imagine) that self-destruction increases the week before Tax Day.

An increase in suicide between our two major holidays, Thanksgiving and Christmas, could have a devastating effect on our national economy.

People who had made plans to kill themselves would spend less on Thanksgiving feasting, which would be felt by the turkey industry, the cranberry industry, and the retail grocery store trade.

Even more serious, large-scale suicides in the middle of December would have a chilling effect, not only on the celebration of Christ's birth, but also on consumer spending.

Consumer spending, you might recall, is what we're depending on to off-set government spending. It's a well established fact that corpses don't spend lavishly at Christmastime. The funeral business might prosper, but most lines such as toys, clothing, and liquor would suffer.

Without a big spurt of consumer spending at Christmas, there is no telling what might happen to the economy, but whatever the result, it would surely demand a tax increase.

And that could lead us into a nasty cycle: more taxes, more

suicides, fewer taxpayers, higher deficits, more inflation—and perhaps even more complicated forms from the IRS which would make suicide a non-deductable item.

It's very complicated, all this tax stuff. With Tax Day on April 15, we can't enjoy springtime, but if Tax Day fell on December 15 it would ruin Thanksgiving and Christmas.

So we can take some comfort in knowing that things could be worse. Still, the question remains, "Could things be better?"

At first glance, the answer seems to be NO. And at second glance, the answer still seems to be NO, the reason being that experience has shown that with taxes, the progression always moves from worse to much worse.

How, then, does a country with our representative form of government reform its tax system? In the late eighteenth century, we reformed the British tax system by going to war and throwing the British into the sea.

One unfortunate result of our victory over the tax-mongering British was that we replaced them with tax-mongering Americans. We threw the rascals out and won for ourselves the precious freedom to elect our own slate of rascals.

Perhaps, instead of trying to reform our tax system, we should concentrate on making the best of it. Because of our tax structure, we now lead the world in the production of million-dollar stud horses. With the proper incentives, we could have Interstate 35 between San Antonio and Oklahoma City solid in horse farms, instead of what it is today—one horse farm every mile.

If we could convince the Russians and Japanese that what their people really need is more stud horses, we just might have this thing licked. We wouldn't need tax reform, only more accountants and more hotrod horses.

A Horse Accident

Tom and I were cowboys. We worked on a ranch in the northern Texas Panhandle, and to us the coming of spring was a special source of joy.

The winter of 1979-80 had been a bear. The ice and snow and cutting winds of January and February had been bad, but the worst part of the winter had come toward the first of March, with a long period of cold rain.

Day after day it had rained. Slow rain, hard rain, rain mixed with snow and sleet, rain driven by a cruel northeast wind.

We had worked out in it every day, wearing yellow slickers and four-buckle overshoes and cowboy hats that were soaked through with water.

But then spring had come, soft days heavy with the scent of green grass and the honking of cranes and geese flying north. And, like cowboys everywhere, we were filled with joy.

The coming of spring meant that we could throw our overshoes in a corner of the saddle house, start practicing with our ropes, and get back to working with colts.

Tom had a bay mare named Bonnie that he had been bringing along since the fall. She was a tall, leggy mare, still green and awkward but eager to please. Tom had been patient with her and had brought her on slowly, and she promised to make a dandy saddle mare.

One evening in April we had to drive a herd of steers several miles across country to a pasture along Wolf Creek. It was easy work, just right for a green horse. Tom gave Bonnie a chance to work cattle, put a light sweat on her, and got her used to dragging a rope.

The sun was slipping toward the horizon when we delivered the steers to the pasture and started back to headquarters. The evening air was delicious with the smells of fresh grass and wild-flowers. It was one of those times when a cowboy feels that he is one of God's chosen people, a lucky man to have been given the chance to follow the horseback life.

We trotted our horses toward home and played with our ropes, throwing at sagebrush and soapweeds. We came to a steep hill that led down to a draw. I was coiling up my rope and happened to be looking at Tom.

Bonnie stumbled in the caliche rock. She staggered several steps, trying to keep her feet. Her chest hit the ground. I kept thinking she would wallow to her feet.

But she couldn't pull out of it. Her head and neck rolled under. I watched in horror as this thousand pound animal tumbled down the hill and began a forward roll.

Tom was still in the stirrups, with the rope in his hands and a stunned expression on his face. I watched Bonnie's back end go up and over. And as Tom saw what was coming, I heard him murmur, "Oh God."

He plunged face-first to the rocky ground, then disappeared beneath the horse. I had seen wrecks before, but I had never seen one that was so certain to crush and cripple a man as this one.

I dived out of the saddle and ran to him, just as the mare rolled off of him. His eyes were closed, his face compressed in pain. I lifted his head off the rocks and cradled it in my arms. I feared that he might be dying.

"It's all right, Tom. Just lie still."

He blinked his eyes. "I can't tell how bad I'm hurt." He tried to sit up.

"Lie still, don't move."

"Got to." He struggled. I thought maybe he was delirious.

"Don't move, Tom."

"Got to. I'm in an ant den."

I stared at him. "*Ant den!* Hell, if you're worried about ants, you ain't hurt very bad." I let his head drop.

Five minutes later, we were ahorseback again. Tom walked funny for a couple of weeks, but he was all right. They say that to kill a genuine cowboy, you have to cut off his head and hide it.

Toys

The making and selling of children's toys is major industry in the United States. Every year toy sales climb into the billions of dollars.

We have three children and we have done our part to support the toy industry. I have never doubted that our children possess more toys than they need or can use, and every time I step on a little bulldozer or a plastic Han Solo in the early morning darkness, I promise myself that I'm going to get control of the situation.

Of course I never do. That's one of those threats you make while the pain is still intense but which you find impossible to carry out in the light of day. What kind of monster would throw out his children's toys? There's probably a law against it anyway.

The sad truth about the toy situation is that in the long run it's simpler to move into a bigger house. Indeed, there may be a direct correlation between toy sales and building permits.

Our youngest child passed the yearling mark last December. He's still a little bow-legged, but he gets around the house very well. He's a sharp little guy and he's old enough now to play with toys, not only the ones he has acquired but also the ones he has inherited from his older brother and sister.

But the interesting thing about little Mark is that he doesn't play with toys. He has a house-full of toys and he won't touch them. Well, all right, he'll touch them. He doesn't mind pulling them out of the toy boxes and closets and out from under Scottie's bed (Scot is nine and still hasn't discovered the toy box in his room).

Yes, Mark will touch his toys, just long enough to trash a room, and then he walks away to find something to play with.

This kid loves empty beer cans. Turn your back on him for a minute and you'll find him in the kitchen garbage, pulling out yesterday's mail order catalogs, now heavy with coffee grounds and bacon grease, and pitching them on the floor, until he finds what he wants: an empty beer can.

He'll fondle it, gnaw on it, carry it around the house, and bang it against the furniture. Or he may drop it into my boot, where I will find it the following morning at 5:30 when I stab a foot into it. Whatever he does with it, a beer can brings joy into his life.

Sometimes I worry about this. Aren't modern kids supposed to fascinated with hi-tech toys that talk and teach? I mean, the boy is past one year old. Shouldn't he be playing with toys that prepare him for the College Boards Examination? *What is he learning from those beer cans?*

There is an old man who goes down our alley every few days. He wears a ruin of a hat and a long gray overcoat, and he carries a gunny sack. He goes through the garbage and salvages aluminum cans.

We're a wasteful culture and I'm glad to see someone making use of what we throw away. But every time I see him shambling down the alley, I can't help thinking of my son and wondering what the old man was playing with sixty years ago . . .

As much as little Mark loves beer cans, they are his second choice. He goes to the garbage only when he's denied access to the bathroom. His first love, his most cherished plaything, is our toilet.

I guess that by the time a guy reaches the age of forty, he has lost much of the mystery and delight of childish discovery. I find it hard to see a toilet as anything but a functional, efficient piece of household equipment. Apparently Mark sees much more than that.

When he began sticking his hands into the pot, we scolded him because, well, it just wasn't sanitary. But then he began putting his whole arm in, soaking his clothes up to the shoulder. And the first time my wife found him standing over the toilet, dipping her toothbrush into the water and then scrubbing his four front teeth, we had "hell among the yearlings," as the cowboys put it.

What is most baffling about this is that the lad has never had more than a sniffle in his entire sixteen months on this earth. While the rest of us have battled colds and allergies, Mark the Water Child has remained as healthy as a horse.

The message here could be that if comode water doesn't kill them within twenty-four hours, they're likely to come away with a very stout resistance to plague and disease. Which doesn't mean that the rest of us will give up orange juice and vitamin C tablets, but it's something to ponder.

Around our house, the sound of water splashing sends heads snapping back and brings Kris or me to our feet. We never know what new horror awaits us at the end of that familiar sprint to the bathroom.

What will be in the toilet this time? A wash cloth? A bar of soap? More toothbrushes? My racketball racket? A hairbrush? My electric razor? The checkbook? One of my manuscripts?

And will we catch that plump little hand before it reaches the flush lever and pulls down, bringing forth a delightful gush of water and a fifty-dollar plumbing bill?

A thousand years from now, some advanced civilization will excavate our sewer line. I would love to be present to hear the report, just to see how archaeologists of another age deduce function from the evidence at hand.

An advanced civilization, by definition, would never allow children around, since children introduce a state of chaos undreamed of by Grendel's mother. So it isn't likely that the scientists of the future will hit upon the right answer: twenty-three pounds of snails, rails, and puppydog tails, a smiling, brown-eyed, curly-headed, bow-legged little human boychild with a strange attraction to beer cans and toilets.

Kris and I still aren't sure how common this is among American children. We keep hoping that Mark will grow up to be a normal, healthy child. We keep thinking that one of these days, he will discover electric trains and trucks and athletics and maybe even the computer toys that will prepare him for college.

It hasn't shown itself yet. We haven't panicked but we're looking around for books on The Beer Can Child. Surely our Mark isn't the first child who turned out . . . uh . . . gifted in this particular area.

If there are others, if there are *many* others, the toy industry could feel the effects. But even if they brought out a line of beer can and comode toys, the kids might reject them too. That would be just like a danged kid, turn his nose up at a $9.95 beer can because it lacked coffee grounds and grease, walk away from a $75 comode toy because it was too clean and socially acceptable.

But the toy industry will survive, if for no other reason because they long ago discovered a piece of ancient wisdom: The people who buy children's toys are adults, not children.

My Race Against
The Golden Palomino

It is March. A bitter wind sweeps across the plains from the southwest and the sky has become a dirty brown. A little while ago, I drove past the high school and saw several hooded figures leaning into the wind. They were on the track team and they were trying to run.

That might have been me, twenty-some years ago. I remember very well the agony of running track in the Panhandle, and one race in particular, when I ran against Donnie Anderson, "The Golden Palomino."

Downstate, March is usually a charming month with fruit trees bursting into bloom and still days that are neither too warm nor too cold. The kind of day, in other words, that makes a young buck want to go out and see how far he can run and jump.

Up here in the north country, we start getting decent running weather about the time track season comes to an end.

In the track season of 1961 I was a tall, skinny kid without any remarkable gifts. At our little 2-A school, if a guy wasn't obviously a sprinter, a weight man, or a jumper, he got stuck in the distance events, the 880 yard run and the mile, which to me sounded a lot like a sentence to Devil's Island.

I was pronounced a half-miler, and in the afternoons I began training with the distance men. Our warmup exercise every day consisted of running "the section," four miles of dirt roads around a section of land west of Perryton.

A blizzard or a cold rain would keep us in the gym, but if the weather was merely bad, we ran the section. If we had any pretty days, I don't remember them. What I remember is stumbling over frozen mud and fighting against the cursed, ever-present wind.

It didn't take much of this frozen road work to convince me that I needed to find another event. I studied on it and came up with only one, the 110 yard high hurdles. It happened that Coach Beck needed depth in that event, so he told me to start working out with the hurdlers.

I could hardly conceal my joy. While the distance men ran the section and pounded out endless laps around the track, the hurdlers worked on sprints, starts, and timing—three-stepping the distance between two hurdles. That was my idea of easy living.

Toward the end of February, we loaded up in "Old Yeller," the school activity bus, and drove to our first track meet, the Greyhound Relays in Gruver, some forty miles away. All the small schools in the Panhandle were there: the Perryton Rangers, the Spearman Lynx, the Stratford Elks, the Gruver Greyhounds, the Dalhart Wolves, the Stinnett Rattlers, the Booker Kiowas, and the Canadian Wildcats.

When we stepped off the bus, we were greeted by a numbing wind. A norther had blown in, just in time for the meet. Dust swirled across the dirt track, hats and papers flew across the football field, school flags and pennants popped like bullwhips, and the tent-headquarters strained at its ropes and threatened to take off at any moment.

We had not dressed for Arctic weather. Over our skimpy uniforms we wore red cotton warmups with hooded tops, which were a small improvement over stark nakedness but not very warm.

With much grumbling and moaning, we climbed off the bus and started running laps to warm up. Going south, we flew.

81

Running north into the wind, we hardly moved.

This was my first track meet. I had run a full flight of high hurdles in practice, where it was just me working on my steps and running against the stopwatch, but I had never run hurdles in competition. I was scared.

When they called flights and lanes, I discovered that I would be running against a kid from Stinnett named Donnie Anderson. We had heard about him. Not only had he just been named first team all-state as a running back, but he was the kind of athlete who won track meets all by himself.

After winning the sprints against the sprinters and the hurdles against the hurdlers, he would go over to the pits and take the jumping events away from the jumpers, and then, if he had time, beat the weight men in the shot put and discus.

This is the same fellow who went on to become an All-America at Texas Tech and played running back for the Green Bay Packers and St. Louis Cardinals. He was a remarkable athlete, and competing against him in high school wasn't fun.

I wasn't worried about beating Donnie. I wanted to make a respectable showing, that's all. I wanted to finish the race before he got out of the showers.

I ran my warmup laps with our star hurdler, Danny Witt. He had run in competition many times and running another flight of hurdles in the Greyhound Relays didn't bother him at all. But I was scared.

After warming up, we started working on our starts. Coming out of the blocks, I was churning my arms, got the draw string of my hood caught around my wrist, and pulled the opening down to a small hole. All at once, I couldn't see.

I yelled for Danny to come help me, just as the public address system crackled and the announcer called the high hurdlers to the starting line. With numb fingers, Danny pulled and tugged at my hood until he finally got me out of it.

We had to hurry over to the starting line. The hurdlers were there, pulling off their warmups and turning blue in the wind. I

caught a glimpse of Donnie Anderson, a big blond kid with thighs like a bullfrog. He was rolling his shoulders. I guess that's all he had to do to warm up for a race.

I pulled off my warmups and shuddered at the cold. The starter called us to the blocks. I stepped into the blocks and looked out at a forest of hurdles, one of the most intimidating spectacles I had ever seen. I only had to jump ten of those 130 hurdles, but I had to find them first.

The starter's gun went up. He called us to our marks. It was then that I realized that something was wrong with my vision. I was seeing two hurdles instead of one. "Get set!" When my hood had closed up, it had knocked one of my contact lenses out of my eye. "Go!" And it was too late to scratch.

I don't think it will hurt Donnie Anderson's reputation if I say that he had lousy form as a hurdler. Me, I worked hard on form. I could shoot my left hand out, touch my right toe, duck my head, and clear a hurdle with only inches to spare. That's the way it's supposed to be done.

Donnie went over a hurdle like a cow hopping a barbed wire fence. I would bet that he never worked it in practice. He had no form, only 9.8 speed between hurdles. I had great form and something like twelve-flat speed between hurdles. When you have 9.8 speed, you don't worry about form.

Donnie and I were nose-to-nose going into the first hurdle, and there we parted. I saw two images instead of one and had to choose to jump one or the other. I picked the wrong one, dug my spikes into the real one, got tangled up in it, staggered into the next lane, knocked that fellow out of the race, and then did a swan dive on the hardest dirt track in Hansford County.

Anderson won the flight and also the event. He had his warmups on and was on his way to the high jump pit by the time I made it across the finish line.

I went home from that frigid track meet minus a lot of skin. Anderson went home with enough blue ribbons to make himself a decent suit of clothes.

84

Coyote Stories

One afternoon in the fall of 1976 I made a windmill run in my pickup. I was managing a 5000 acre ranch in the sandhill country north of the Beaver River in the Oklahoma Panhandle, and I had 9 Dempster mills on the place.

It was a hot, still October day, just right for climbing up a windmill tower, oiling the head, and tightening fan bolts. I was driving along a lease road when I saw something move out in the pasture.

At first I thought it was a dog. I pulled off the road and drove toward it. As I drew closer, I saw that it was a half-grown coyote. Instead of running from me, as he should have, he staggered and fell, got up and staggered some more.

He couldn't run and could hardly walk. I figured he had rabies, and if I had had a gun I would have shot him. But I didn't have a gun, so I watched him for a while.

I noticed some coyote droppings in the grass, and I got out and looked at them. They were composed almost entirely of *tunas*, the fruit of our small northern variety of cactus. That pup wasn't sick, he was about to starve to death.

I guessed that he was a spring pup and had been kicked out of the den to make his way in the world. The fact that his droppings contained no trace of grasshoppers, mice, rabbits, or ground squirrels indicated that he hadn't learned to hunt. Maybe he had lost his mother over the summer, or maybe he just hadn't paid attention in hunting class.

Whatever the reason, he was about finished and in no condition to get the protein he needed to stay alive.

Now, I wasn't sentimental about coyotes. I enjoyed having them on the ranch and hearing them sing in the evenings and early mornings, yet I recognized that we were on opposites sides of the law, so to speak.

As long as they ate rodents and carrion, we could share the ranch and get along just fine. If they started killing calves, and they had on a few occasions, I used traps and a .30-.30 to thin them out.

My friendship with the coyote population was based on Old Testament justice: "eye for eye, tooth for tooth."

I should have driven off and let nature finish what she had started. But the coyotes hadn't been bothering the cattle and here was this helpless pup . . .

Maybe when a guy gets a little age on him, has a couple of kids at home and has spent a few horseback hours thinking about life and death, he begins to lose his taste for killing. All life is a wonder and a miracle, whether it's an ant or coyote or a little boy playing on the front porch.

That coyote pup was on the wrong side of the law, but I couldn't see that the world would be much improved if I let him starve.

I had a catch rope with me in the pickup. I built a little calf-size loop, walked up to the pup, and stuck it on him. I thought he might chew my rope but he didn't. I reeled him in and threw him in the back of the pickup.

On the way back to the house, I felt a little ashamed of myself and I sure was hoping I didn't meet my neighbor on the road. Mark *hated* coyotes, and not without reason. A couple of winters ago a crippled she-coyote had made a real good living stalking his first-calf heifers.

Before he finally caught up with her and killed her, she put a dent in his calf crop. She was a smart old gal, too smart for her own good. She had watched the heifers long enough to know that when one went down in labor, she couldn't protect her calf.

The old coyote would wait near the heifer's tail and kill the calf as soon as it came out. Then she would leave, watch from a distance, and return to the kill when the heifer went to water or abandoned the calf.

G. L. Holmes

If a guy saw that a time or two, it might sour his attitude about coyotes.

Well, there I was trucking a coyote home and feeling more than a little guilty about it and hoping that Mark was out ahorseback or on top of a windmill tower.

I made it home without getting caught and I stuck the pup in an old dog kennel that hadn't been used in many years. It had a cement floor and a cyclone fence around it and a wooden doghouse at one end.

Even though I had decided the pup wasn't rabid, I didn't intend to take any chances. I shot a jackrabbit and threw it in the kennel. I would give the pup two days to eat. If he didn't, I would assume he was sick and shoot him.

Two days later the rabbit was gone and the pup had begun to look a bit more prosperous.

I kept him around and fed him whatever I could scrounge up — scraps, rabbits, a few packages of freezer-burned hamburger.

I don't know what the pup did at night, whether he came out of the dog house and paced around the cage, but during the day I never saw him outside. Now and then when I got caught up on my work, I would go into the kennel and watch him.

When I got into the pen with him, I wore heavy gloves and went armed with a piece of pipe. I didn't know how he would respond to my presence.

His response was entirely passive. When he saw that he couldn't escape and that I intended to stay for a while, he just sat there like a statue. He never growled or showed his teeth.

I was curious to see if he would respond to kindness, the way a dog would, and after I had stood within three feet of him on several occasions, I moved closer and petted him.

Even though I was wearing a heavy welding glove, this wasn't very smart. Later, I heard about a rancher up on the Cimarron who picked up what he thought was a dead coyote and got bitten on the hand.

88

The bite itself wasn't so bad but he got blood poisoning from it, spent a week in the hospital, and almost lost his hand.

But I was curious and I had to try petting the coyote. The answer to my question, would he respond to kind treatment, was no. He showed no response, no emotion, nothing. When I touched him, he cringed but didn't move. He just sat there, rigid.

One thing I noticed about the pup was that when I appeared at the door of the kennel, he would watch me from inside the dog house. He never took his eyes off me. But when I got up close, he never looked at me with a direct gaze.

I thought that was interesting. A dog will look you in the eye unless you're mad at him, and then he might look away. But this little fellow wouldn't look straight at me, even when I moved and talked and tried to get his attention.

Well, I kept him around for a couple of weeks and enjoyed the opportunity to watch a coyote at close range. But when he got his strength back, I figured it was time to let him go back to the wild and learn some hunting tricks before the snow started to fly.

One evening I left the door open. I also left a package of old hamburger nearby, just to see if he would hang around.

The next morning the pup was nowhere in sight, and neither was the hamburger. I kept leaving food out and it kept disappearing. Though I never saw him around the place during the day, I figured he was staying pretty close and coming back at night.

Then one morning I found him dead in the road. It appeared that he had been run over by a car or truck. A couple of days later I ran into Mark, who knew the rest of the story.

He said he had been driving to town one evening around sundown and had spotted a coyote sitting beside the road near our house. Coming back late that night, he saw the same coyote sitting in the middle of the road.

Well, Mark wasn't one to pass up an opportunity to cull the coyote population, and he ran him down. When he finished telling his story, I told him mine. He was surprised, and I think he felt kind of bad about it. Naturally he hadn't realized that I had made a research project out of the pup, because I hadn't wanted to tell him.

I didn't blame Mark for what he'd done. After the market wreck of 1974, it had been hard to make a living in the cattle business, and calf-killing coyotes had only compounded the problem. His bad feelings about coyotes had something to do with the fact that he was trying to make a living for a wife and three kids, and to hold the ranch together.

I guess what made me sad about the experience was that in the process of trying to help a wild animal, I had dulled his survival instincts and made him into a welfare client who couldn't make it in either world.

Nature has its own rules. Sometimes they seem harsh to us humans and we're tempted to intervene and tamper with them. But when we do, most of the time it doesn't work out very well.

I thought that was the end of it. But the following spring, Mark showed up at my spring branding with an unusual gift. Out of the pocket of his blue jean jacket he pulled a little black puppy and handed it to me.

We already had two dogs, the kind most cowboys own and wish they didn't. They were sincere but utterly worthless. We didn't need another.

But before I could turn it down, I noticed a couple of odd things about this pup. For one thing, he bit me on the thumb. He wasn't big enough to do any damage, since he just barely had his eyes open, but he was pretty serious about it nevertheless.

That was strange. Most pups that age are either friendly or passive. Not this one. He wanted to bite, and he had a pretty impressive set of milk teeth. They were as sharp as needles, and even though they didn't break the skin, they got my attention.

Then I noticed that the pup was trying to growl, and that his eyes were an unusual color, a deep, smoky gray.

Mark laughed and told me that what I held in my hand was a coyote pup, not a dog pup.

90

"I dug him out of a den yesterday," he said. "I owe you one and I thought you might want him."

Well yes, I did. I had a natural curiosity about coyotes and had never raised one from a pup. I figured it would be an interesting experiment.

I could hardly wait to introduce the pup to our two dogs. They were both females and had raised so many litters of mongrel pups, I was sure this one would arouse their maternal instincts.

That evening, after the roundup, I called them up to the porch. Maybe they were suspicious from the start, since I called them in a sweet tone of voice. They were accustomed to being yelled at, you see, and for the very best of reasons: they were registered Goofoffs and they were always in trouble for something or other.

They came up to the porch, grinning as dogs do, wagging their tails, and looking guilty. I set the pup down in front of them. They stared, exchanged glances, and began to sniff the little ball of fur.

The little ball of fur began to growl and bit Foxie on the nose. The dogs left in a hurry. I managed to catch Foxie and tried to coax her back. No deal. She didn't know what that thing was that had bit her on the nose, and she didn't want to know.

I slipped my hand under her collar and tried to lead her back to the pup. She locked down all four legs and I had to sled her across the cement porch. I tried to explain that I had a new puppy for her to adopt and told her how much fun they could have together.

Foxie wasn't too bright but she had already figured this deal out. That Thing didn't smell or act like any pup she had ever produced, and she wanted nothing to do with it.

When I released her collar, she shot off the porch and spent the rest of the day down in the stack lot. She didn't get within rifle range of the pup from then on.

So my plan for adopting the coyote off on the dogs fell flat. And after the pup had been around the house for a couple of days,

I began to think that, for once, my dogs had made a sensible, intelligent decision.

Even though the little villain looked cute, he wasn't. He had a nasty disposition that stayed nasty. He would not only bite the hand that fed him, he would bite any hand. Or foot. Or anything that was warm and moved.

I could have put up with this myself, but little Scottie was three years old at that time and his mother wanted him to grow up with all his fingers and a minimum of scar tissue.

After a week, it appeared that we would have to get rid of Scottie or the coyote. We decided to keep Scot. The coyote had to go.

It happened that a cousin of mine from California showed up at the ranch about that time. Paul had grown up in suburban Los Angeles, and he was infatuated with everything he saw on the ranch.

He wanted to ride horses, chase cattle, shoot guns, wear boots, and drive in mud. I knew he was green when he showed me a gun he had bought in Amarillo. It was an ancient rolling-block rifle of some outrageous caliber, something like .48-.20.

The shell was about the size of your big toe and it threw enough lead to knock the side out of a barn—if you could have hit a barn, which you couldn't because that fat hunk of lead began dropping the instant it left the muzzle.

That's why nobody used .48-.20 any more, because it was only slightly more accurate than a hand-thrown brick. And that's why Paul had gotten a good deal on the gun.

But he was proud of it, and he told me how, on his way out to the ranch, he had seen a bunch of wild turkeys on the highway and had stopped and opened fire on them.

He was disappointed that he had missed, but I told him not to feel too badly about it since wild turkeys shot on state highways, out of season and without a license, were worth about $500 and ten days in jail if the game warden found out about it.

He seemed surprised.

Well, Cousin Paul fell in love with the wide open spaces and ranch life, and he fell in love with my coyote pup. A plan began to take shape in my mind.

The day Paul left for Los Angeles, I said, "How would you like to take a coyote pup back with you?"

He looked at me with astonishment, and that's when I realized that I could have *sold* him the pup and he still would have been delighted. But he was family. And anyway, he didn't have any money.

I gave him the pup and made him the happiest kid in the whole western United States. He promised to honor and protect it and give it a good decent home. In suburban Los Angeles.

When Cousin Paul and his new pet pulled away from the ranch, my wife and I looked at each other and smiled, remembered the follies of our youth, and looked forward to hearing the next chapter of the coyote story.

We didn't hear the rest of the story for a long time. Years later, when Cousin Paul was older and wiser and able to laugh about it, he told us.

Driving across country, he put the coyote in the front seat with him and tried to make friends. Paul played. The coyote bit, hard.

But they made it to L.A., moved into Paul's house, and fell into a normal routine. The coyote stayed in the house much of the time, even though he wasn't exactly house-broke, and roamed the neighborhood when Paul let him out.

One evening Paul decided to splurge. He went to the store and bought a sack of charcoal and a whole chicken. He had his taste buds set on some old-fashioned barbecued chicken.

He started the fire and went inside to cut up the chicken. He unwrapped it and set it on the counter and moved a few steps away to find a sharp knife.

In that short length of time, his coyote, who had been watching it all with keen interest, leaped up on the counter, snatched the chicken up in his jaws, jumped to the floor, and ran

93

out the screen door.

When Paul saw what had happened, he ran out the door and chased the coyote around the neighborhood, trying to get his chicken back. He didn't. Only later did he wonder what the neighbors thought of this spectacle—a grown man with a butcher knife, running after a half-grown coyote with a whole chicken in his mouth, in a quiet neighborhood in suburban Los Angeles.

This may have been Paul's first clue that maybe I hadn't done him a favor in giving him the coyote.

It wasn't long after this that Paul began hearing rumors from people on the block. Something strange was going on. All at once, and for no apparent reason, pet cats that had never strayed from home were just disappearing. No clues, no suspects, nothing. They just vanished.

Hardly a cat remained in a neighborhood that had had dozens of them.

Paul allowed as how this was indeed strange, and began keeping his coyote in the yard. The depredations ceased just as mysteriously as they had begun.

The final chapter of the saga of Cousin Paul and his coyote occurred a few months later. Paul decided it was time to improve the appearance of his house. He had furnished the place with whatever he could borrow from relatives and buy cheap at the Goodwill Store.

He saved up his money and bought a nice sofa. He put it in the livingroom and was pleased that it changed the looks of the place, made it look more like a home and less like a bunkhouse.

One evening he went out to eat and left his coyote inside the house. When he came home, he found sofa-stuffing all over the front room. The coyote had dug a den right in the middle of the new sofa and had moved in.

That was enough, even for Paul. He loaded up the coyote, drove out into the hills, and turned him loose, to make his way in the world with his own kind.

I guess that was a hard way of learning that you can take a coyote out of the country, but you can't take the country out of a coyote. He may *look* like a dog, but there are important differences.

G. L. Holmes

John R. Erickson is the author of 15 books and hundreds of articles. His work has appeared in the *Dallas Times Herald, Texas Highways, Western Horseman, Persimmon Hill, The Cattleman, Livestock Weekly,* and many other places. He is a member of the Texas Institute of Letters, the Philosophical Society of Texas, the Western Writers of America. He lives in Perryton, Texas, with his wife Kristine and their three children.

Drawings by Gerald L. Holmes have appeared in *Beef Magazine, Western Horseman, The Cattleman,* and other places. He has published one book of cartoons, *Pickens County,* and his work has illustrated ten of John Erickson's books. He lives on a farm near Perryton, Texas, with his wife Carol and their two sons.

The typeface used in this book is Palatino; printed by Cushing-Malloy, Inc., Ann Arbor, Michigan.

Designed and produced by Word Services, 1927 S. 26th, Lincoln, Nebraska 68502.

MORE GREAT ENTERTAINMENT
BY JOHN ERICKSON

ACE REID: COWPOKE

Ace Reid: Cowpoke by John R. Erickson. Photographs and cartoons. Index. #17A clothbound $15.95.

This biography is a milestone in western writing, for it brings together two of the most popular humorists of our day: Ace Reid and John Erickson. When these two cowboys get together,the result is a book you won't be able to put down.

Ace Reid Cowpokes Cartoon Books, Set of 7. #S08. $24.95.

Ace Reid's cartoons have been a staple in the literature of the West for the past 30 years, and we're proud to offer this shrink-wrapped set of 7 of his best cartoon collections. This set is a great companion for John Erickson's biography, *Ace Reid: Cowpoke.*

The HANK THE COWDOG Series of Books
by John R. Erickson
Drawings by Gerald L. Holmes

Hank the Cowdog. #1A paperback $5.95. # 1B hardcover $9.95.

The Further Adventures of Hank the Cowdog. #2A paperback $5.95. #2B hardback $9.95.

It's a Dog's Life. #3A paperback $5.95. #3B hardcover $9.95.

Murder in the Middle Pasture. #4A paperback $5.95. #4A hardcover $9.95.

Faded Love. #5A paperback $5.95. #5B hardcover $9.95.

Let Sleeping Dogs Lie.. #6A paperback $5.95. #6B hardcover $9.95.

The Curse of the Incredible Priceless Corn Cob. (September 1986) #7A paperback $5.95. #7B hardcover $9.95.

JOHN R. ERICKSON'S
STORIES ON CASSETTE TAPE

Hank the Cowdog. #1C tapeset $13.95. (2 cassettes)

The Further Adventures of Hank the Cowdog. #2C tapeset $13.95. (2 cassettes)

It's a Dog's Life. #3C tapeset $13.95. (2 cassettes)

Murder in the Middle Pasture. #4C tapeset $13.95. (2 cassettes)

Faded Love. #5C tapeset $13.95. (2 cassettes)

Let Sleeping Dogs Lie.. #6C tapeset $13.95. (2 cassettes)

The Curse of the Incredible Priceless Corn Cob. (September 1986) #7C tapeset $13.95. (2 cassettes)

Hank the Cowdog's Greatest Hits. #21C tape $6.95.

The Devil in Texas and Other Cowboy Tales. #22C tapeset $13.95. (2 cassettes)

MORE GREAT BOOKS
BY JOHN R. ERICKSON

Cowboy Country. (September 1986) Photographs by Kris Erickson. #18B hardback $15.95.

The Hunter. (fiction) #16B hardback $11.95.

The Modern Cowboy. Photographs by Kris Erickson. #15A paperback $6.95.

Panhandle Cowboy. Photographs by Bill Ellzey. #13A paperback $5.95.

COWBOY HUMOR
BY JOHN R. ERICKSON

Cowboys Are A Separate Species. #24A paperback $5.95. #24B hardback $9.95.

The Devil in Texas and Other Cowboy Tales. #P04 paperback $5.95.

Cowboys Are Partly Human. #10A paperback $5.95. #10B hardback $9.95.

Alkali County Tales. #11A paperback $5.95. #11B hardback $9.95.

Alkali County Tales

The Devil In Texas

Cowboys Are Partly Human

MAVERICK BOOKS ORDER FORM

Spring 1986

Name _____

Address _____

City _____ State _____ Zip _____

Visa/MasterCharge # _____ Expires _____

Item #	Description	Price	Quantity	Total

Subtotal _____

*Enclose $1 postage & handling per paperback $2 postage per hardback

Postage* _____

**Texas residents include 5⅛% (.05125) sales tax.

Sales Tax** _____

Total _____

Maverick Books, Inc., Box 549, Perryton, Texas 79070 / (806) 435-7611